JOHN ERMINE OF THE YELLOWSTONE

John Ermine

JOHN ERMINE OF THE YELLOWSTONE

FREDERIC REMINGTON

ILLUSTRATED BY FREDERIC REMINGTON

INTRODUCTION BY ROBERT L. DORMAN

BARNES & NOBLE

NEW YORK

CONTENTS

LIST OF ILLUSTRATIONS

INTRODUCTION

WITH *JOHN ERMINE OF THE YELLOWSTONE*, FIRST PUBLISHED IN 1902, artist Frederic Remington captured his vision of the Old West in words rather than paint and bronze. Set against the dramatic backdrop of the Indian wars, it is the tragic story of a man caught between two racial worlds, the Native American tribe in which he had been raised and the white civilization that he serves in its mission of conquest. Featuring the author's own illustrations, *John Ermine* offers a vivid depiction of frontier army life as well as a classic tale of unrequited love. It was the last work of fiction that Remington wrote and remains his most enduring literary achievement, helping to establish the western as a favorite of modern American readers.

Although he will forever be identified with the American West, Frederic Remington (1861–1909) was born in Canton, New York, near the St. Lawrence River. He attended military schools as a youth and discovered his artistic talent by sketching soldiers and fellow cadets. From 1878 to 1880, Remington studied art and played football at Yale, but dropped out after the untimely death of his father, a Civil War veteran whom he revered. In 1881, Remington made the first of his many trips to the West, visiting the site of the recent Battle of the Little Bighorn. He sold his first western-themed illustration to *Harper's Weekly* magazine in 1886 and soon became one of the most sought-after illustrators in the country, published regularly in major national magazines. Remington provided illustrations for his own articles and stories as well as those of leading writers on the West like Theodore Roosevelt and Owen Wister. He accompanied the army's expeditions against Geronimo in 1886 and the Sioux in 1890, and in 1898 he traveled to Cuba to cover the Spanish-American War. Besides producing many acclaimed paintings and sculptures during his foreshortened career, Remington also published eight books, including the fiction collection *Sundown Leflare* in 1899 and his first novel, *The Way of an Indian*, which was written in 1900 but did not appear until 1905. In 1902, Remington wrote and published *John Ermine of the Yellowstone* in three furious months as a rejoinder to Owen Wister's best-selling western *The Virginian* (1902), which he considered to be too romantic and unrealistic. Afterwards, Remington abandoned fiction writing to focus on painting and sculpting until his death from appendicitis in 1909. His portrayal of the West has influenced artists, writers, and filmmakers down to the present.

What annoyed Remington most about Wister's *The Virginian* was its happy ending. His own vision of the West was essentially tragic. All of the heroic types that the frontier had created, and which Remington sought to immortalize in oils and bronze—the cowboy, the cavalry soldier, the Indian brave—were fleeting, he believed, soon to be civilized out of existence. In *The Virginian*, the title character is a drawling Southerner who is a natural aristocrat, a born leader of men despite his humble origins. But his superiority in the frontier Wyoming setting, governed by the rugged code of the West, is challenged by the arrival of the genteel New England schoolmarm, who represents the advent of modern civilization. In the end, the two are married, and the implication is that the Virginian will adapt and prosper in the post-frontier world of railroads, commerce, and manners. This reading somewhat oversimplified Wister's plot, but it was Remington's reading. He rejected the possibility that the frontiersman could exist outside the ephemeral circumstances of frontier freedom and lawlessness. He must ride into the sunset and perish.

To make this argument in *John Ermine*, Remington chose to inject *race* into the scenario, ostensibly an absolute category in the minds of turn-of-the-last-century Americans. If put into racial terms, the transition from frontier to civilization would seem to be unbridgeable. His novel's hero, John Ermine, is a young white man who was raised by Crow (Apsáalooke) Indians under the name of White Weasel and sees himself fully as Native American—"my Indian heart," as Ermine refers to himself. After being apprenticed to an oracular white recluse named Crooked-Bear, who teaches him the basics of European-American culture including English, Ermine volunteers to serve as a scout for the U.S. Army. He functions well in the setting of the army camp, displaying his own natural superiority, until the arrival of the commander's daughter, Katherine Searles. His efforts to woo her end not in marriage but in tragedy. The Native American world that produced formidable hunter-warriors like John Ermine, Remington insists, must vanish in a West made safe for the commander's daughter. Realistically, men like Ermine were too hardened, fierce, and violent to live among decent people. Wister's Virginian—who lynched his best friend and later killed his nemesis in a gunfight on his wedding day—was no different.

Remington's racial views were not very logical, as they rarely are, but they were typical of the era. John Ermine was Caucasian, yet he was brought up as a Crow. What was he? It was the perennial "nature versus nurture" debate: is the self fixed and innate, or is it the product of its environment? To this day, Americans continue to struggle with the issue of racial identity, and in more recent decades some classic works of western fiction and film have explored the theme with regard to white captives or adoptees of Native Americans, including director John Ford's masterpiece *The Searchers* (1956) and novelist Thomas Berger's *Little Big Man* (1964). In his own novel, Remington at first emphasized the captive Ermine's whiteness: "He was born white, but he had a Crow heart, so the tribesmen persuaded themselves. They did not understand the laws of heredity." Remington also seemed to imply that Ermine's white, northern European racial makeup accounted for his superiority over his fellow Crows, which would have been in accord with the mainstream belief in a hierarchy of races with whites at the top. The social science of the time saw this hierarchy as the product of evolution; races in the upper ranks were more advanced than the primitives at the lower levels. However, those primitive or "savage" races, like Native Americans, were in the present-day much like white Europeans must have been in ancient times, as anthropologist Lewis Henry Morgan argued in his influential book *Ancient Society* (1877). Yet some believed, as did Remington, that there remained a latent racial essence that linked white Anglo-Saxons (particularly males) back to their savage forbearers. Under the right circumstances, such as an encounter with primitives or primitive conditions, this deeper racial nature—hardy, lusty, warlike—could be released. "The slumbering untamed Saxon awoke in him"—so it was described in Wister's landmark 1895 article, "The Evolution of the Cow-Puncher," partly ghost-written by Remington during their previous years of collaboration.[1] To Remington's mind, Wister betrayed this atavistic racial ideal when his Virginian married the schoolmarm and became a pillar of the community. He would have none of that for John Ermine. Despite the fact that "all the race had evolved" and an "interval of many centuries intervened between him and his fellows," Ermine still displayed the "qualities of mind which distinguished his remote ancestors of the north of Europe" even after living among civilized whites at the army camp.

Wister actually was closer to popular attitudes regarding the experience of the primitive, as the booming sales of his novel revealed. Indeed, when *John Ermine* was adapted to the stage in 1903, it was refitted with a happier ending. (Remington privately fumed about this, but the play closed after a short run in any event; a 1917 silent movie version had yet another alternate ending.) Americans wanted to believe that one could descend to the level of the savage, release one's blood thirst and urge for conquest, then return to civilization and resume normal life. The experience was thought to be rejuvenating, for the individual and the race as a whole, and in American literature the theme already enjoyed a tradition reaching back to James Fenimore Cooper's *Leatherstocking Tales* of the 1820s. This paradoxical desire to domesticate the primitive grew in significance as the daily lives of middle-class Americans became more urbanized and bureaucratized by the turn of the century. It was expressed in diverse ways, from the increasing popularity of hunting, camping, and other forms of outdoor recreation, to President Roosevelt's call to pursue the "strenuous life," including imperial adventures abroad.

The budding wilderness preservation movement, led by John Muir, owed something to it, as did the creation of such youth organizations as the Woodcraft Indians (1902) and the Boy Scouts of America (1910). Better yet, the primitive could also be experienced vicariously, by consumerism. Middle-class shoppers could adorn their homes with authentic Native American crafts purchased at big city department stores, which became all the rage by the late 1890s. And they made best sellers of later novels in the vein of *John Ermine*, including Jack London's *The Call of the Wild* (1903) and Edgar Rice Burroughs' *Tarzan of the Apes* (1914).

Yet if this white middle-class urge toward the primitive was ultimately linked to a pervasive belief in an innate racial character, the other side of the nature-nurture coin was also making strong inroads on social attitudes during this period. The early 1900s, after all, encompassed the Progressive reform era, when numerous initiatives were launched nationally to improve public health, education, and living conditions. This growing appreciation of the shaping power of environment, both social and natural, was rooted in the evolutionary idea that organisms adapt and respond to their environment. Its impact was manifested not just in reform efforts but throughout American culture. Historian Frederick Jackson Turner made one of the most famous applications of it with his "frontier thesis," which held that the individualistic and democratic traits defining America's national character, and differentiating it from Europe, were the product of western frontier conditions. Remington shared this view of history, and he was just as concerned as Turner about the closing of the frontier and what it boded for the nation's future character. His art celebrated the army soldiers and cowboys who were the instruments of this process, but Remington also strongly felt the poignancy of Native Americans and their lost world, which he had attempted to depict in his earlier novel, *The Way of an Indian*. With *John Ermine*, he seemed to be trying to personify the end of the frontier as a tragedy for both races involved. But to create this conflicted character, he must assert the predominance of Ermine's Native American upbringing over his white race. He hedged on this point, clinging to the notion of a primordial white racial core. "But Ermine is not an

Indian," the British hunter Harding asserts to the mixed-blood scout Wolf-Voice, who responds, "Na, but she all de same Engun" "which was true so far as that worthy could see," Remington comments. In any case, after the imprint that the frontier environment has left on him, Ermine cannot simply segue into civilized society, all of his Nordic features and blond locks notwithstanding. "Good-by, good-by, white men, and good-by, white woman," he begins a soliloquy as he leaves behind the army camp. The final chapter of the book is entitled "The End of All Things."

Native Americans might have considered this intense nostalgia of Remington's to be crocodile tears, yet it drove his art. There may have been a time when he was somewhat more sanguine about the passing frontier. In one of his earliest articles, "Horses of the West" (1889), he had displayed much the same ambivalence about heredity versus environment as in *John Ermine*, which he then applied to horse breeds. "To this day the pony of western America shows many points of the [ancestral] Barbary horse to the exclusion of all other breeding," he wrote. "He has borne the Moor, the Spanish conqueror, the red Indian, the mountain-man, and the vaquero through all the glories of their careers." This "equine ideal" set the standard of "worth and beauty and speed," Remington believed, but he also admitted that over time the animal had undergone a "gradual adjustment to his environment" in the West. With the frontier disappearing, Remington seemed to recognize that the horse must make the transition to civilization: "There are no more worlds for him to conquer; now he must till the ground."[2]

Remington was less and less at peace with this conclusion as the years passed, culminating with the defiant gesture of *John Ermine*. Some scholars have suggested that this defiance was linked to his discovery of sculpture, which reinforced his pursuit of the timeless ideal. They note that he took up sculpting for the first time while collaborating with Wister on "The Evolution of the Cow-Puncher," with its ageless archetype of the man on horseback. In letters to Wister and others, Remington proclaimed the imperishable qualities of bronze as opposed to paint or print. His sculptures were often frozen moments of time, capturing an instant of rapid motion, as in his first work, *The Bronco Buster* (1895), or in *Coming Through the Rye* (1902), the sculpture that he was completing in the period when he wrote *John Ermine*. With bronze he might transcend history, change, and loss. At the very least, there was aesthetic satisfaction to fill the painful void of nostalgia. *Coming Through the Rye*, with its racing horsemen firing pistols in the air, was one of Remington's most exuberant sculptures, quite in counterpoint to the tone of *John Ermine*. Remington also returned to painting in a serious way during his final years, experimenting with his technique and ultimately producing some of the best work of his career. He still depicted the West, but many of his pictures were now night scenes. So was the conclusion to *John Ermine*, which opens with the words, "The time for 'taps' was drawing near. . . ."

Robert L. Dorman, Ph.D., is monographs librarian and associate professor at Oklahoma City University. He is the author of *Revolt of the Provinces: The Regionalist Movement in America, 1920–1945*.

JOHN ERMINE OF THE YELLOWSTONE

CHAPTER ONE

VIRGINIA CITY

O NE FINE MORNING IN THE FALL OF '64 ALDER Gulch rolled up its shirt sleeves and fell to the upheaving, sluicing, drifting, and cradling of the gravel. It did not feel exactly like old-fashioned everyday work to the muddy, case-hardened diggers. Each man knew that by evening he would see the level of dust rise higher in his long buckskin gold-bags. All this made for the day when he could retire to the green East and marry some beautiful girl—thereafter having nothing to do but eat pie and smoke fragrant cigars in a basking sunshine of no-work. Pie up at Kustar's bakeshop was now one dollar a pie, and a pipe full of molasses and slivers was the best to be had in the market. Life was hard at Alder in those days—it was practical; and when its denizens became sentimental, it took these unlovely forms, sad to relate.

Notwithstanding the hundreds who toiled in the gulches, Virginia City itself held hurrying crowds—Mormon freighters, pack trains, ponies, dirty men off the trails, wan pilgrims, Indians, Chinese, and almost everything else not angelic.

Into this bustle rode Rocky Dan, who, after dealing faro all night at the "Happy Days" shebang, had gone for a horseback ride through the hills to brighten his eyes and loosen his nerves. Reining up before this place, he tied his pony where a horse-boy from the livery corral could find it. Striding into that unhallowed hall of Sheol, he sang out, "Say, fellers, I've just seen a thing out in the hills which near knocked me off'en my horse. You couldn't guess what it was nohow. I don't believe half what I see and nothin' what I read, but it's out thar in the hills, and you can go throw your eyes over it yourselves."

"What? A new thing, Dan? No! No! Dan, you wouldn't come here with anything good and blurt it out," said the rude patrons of the "Happy Days" mahogany, vulturing about Rocky Dan, keen for anything new in the way of gravel.

"I gamble it wa'n't a murder—that wouldn't knock you off'en your horse, jus' to see one—hey, Dan?" ventured another.

"No, no," vouched Dan, laboring under an excitement ill becoming a faro-dealer. Recovering himself, he told the bartender to "perform his function." The "valley tan" having been disposed of, Dan added:

"It was a boy!"

"Boy—boy—a boy?" sighed the crowd, setting back their "empties." "A boy ain't exactly new, Dan," added one.

"No, that's so," he continued, in his unprofessional perplexity, "but this was a white boy."

"Well, that don't make him any newer," vociferated the crowd.

"No, d—— it, but this was a white boy out in that Crow Injun camp, with yeller hair braided down the sides of his head, all the same Injun, and he had a bow and arrer, all the same Injun; and I said, 'Hello, little feller,' and he pulled his little bow on me, all the same Injun. D—— the little cuss, he was about to let go on me. I was too near them Injuns, anyhow, but I was on the best quarter horse in the country, as you know, and willin' to take my chance. Boys, he was white as Sandy McCalmont there, only he didn't have so many freckles." The company regarded the designated one, who promptly blushed, and they gathered the idea that the boy was a decided blonde.

"Well, what do you make of it, anyhow, Dan?"

"What do I make of it? Why, I make of it that them Injuns has lifted that kid from some outfit, and that we ought to go out and bring him in. He don't belong there, nohow, and that's sure."

"That's so," sang the crowd as it surged into the street; "let's saddle up and go and get him. Saddle up! Saddle up!"

The story blew down the gulch on the seven winds. It appealed to the sympathies of all white men, and with double force to their hatred of the Indians. There was no man at Alder Gulch, even the owners of squaws—and they were many—who had not been given cause for this resentment. Business was suspended. Wagoners cut out and mounted team-horses; desperadoes, hardened roughs, trooped in with honest merchants and hardy miners as the strung-out cavalcade poured up the road to the plateau, where the band of Crows had pitched their tepees.

"Klat-a-way! Klat-a-way!" shouted the men as they whipped and spurred up the steeps. The road narrowed near the top, and here the surging horsemen were stopped by a few men who stood in the middle waving and howling "Halt!" The crowd had no definite scheme of procedure at any time—it was simply impelled forward by the ancient war-shout of *A rescue! A rescue!* The blood of the mob had mounted high, but it drew restive rein before a big man who had forced his pony up on the steep hillside and was speaking in a loud, measured, and authoritative voice.

The riders felt the desire for council; the ancient spirit of the witenagemote came over them. The American town meeting, bred in their bones and burned into their brains, made them listen to the big temporary chairman with the yellow lion's mane blowing about his head in the breeze. His horse did not want to stand still on the perilous hillside, but he held him there and opened.

"Gentlemen, if this yar outfit goes a-chargin' into that bunch of Injuns, them Injuns aforesaid is sure goin' to shoot at us, and we are naturally goin' to shoot back at them. Then, gentlemen, there will be a fight, they will get a bunch of us, and we will wipe them out. Now, our esteemed friend yer, Mr. Chick-chick, savvies Injuns, as you know, he bein' somewhat their way hisself—allows that they will chill that poor little boy with a knife the first rattle out of

The Chairman

the box. So, gentlemen, what good does it all do? Now, gentlemen, I allows if you all will keep down yer under the hill and back our play, Chick-chick and me will go into that camp and get the boy alive. If these Injuns rub us out, it's your move. All what agrees to this motion will signify it by gettin' down off'en their horses."

Slowly man after man swung to the ground. Some did not so readily agree, but they were finally argued off their horses. Whereat the big chairman sang out: "The ayes have it. Come on, Mr. Chick-chick."

These two rode up the hill and over the mesa, trotting along as they talked. "Now, Chick-chick, I don't know a heap about Injuns. The most that I have seen of them was over the sights of a rifle. How are we goin' at this? Do you *habla* Crow lingo, Señor?"

"No," replied that much mixed-blooded man, "I no *cumtux* Crow, but I make the hand talk, and I can clean up a *ten-ass Chinook;* all you do is to do nothing—you no shake hands, you say nothing, until we smoke the pipe, then you say 'How?' and shake hands all same white man. You hang on to your gun—suppose they try take it away—well, den, *icta-nica-ticki,* you shoot! Then we are dead." Having laid his plan of campaign before his brother in arms, no more was said. History does not relate what was thought about it.

They arrived in due course among the tepees of a small band of Crows. There were not probably a hundred warriors present, but they were all armed, horsed, and under considerable excitement. These Crows were at war with all the other tribes of the northern plains, but maintained a truce with the white man. They had very naturally been warned of the unusual storm of horsemen bearing in their direction, and were apprehensive concerning it. They scowled at the chairman and Mr. Chick-chick, who was an Oregon product, as they drew up. The latter began his hand-language, which was answered at great length. He did not at once calm the situation, but was finally invited to smoke in the council lodge. The squaws were pulling down the tepees; roping, bundling, screaming, hustling ponies, children, and dogs about, unsettling the statesmen's nerves mightily as they passed the pipe. The big chairman began to fancy the Indians he had seen through the sights more than these he was regarding over the pipe of peace. Chick-chick gesticulated the proposition that the white papoose be brought into the tent, where he could be seen.

The Indians demurred, saying there was no white boy—that all in the camp were Crows. A young warrior from outside broke into their presence, talking in a loud tone. An old chief looked out through the entrance-flap, across the yellow plains. Turning, he inquired what the white horsemen were doing outside.

He was told that they wanted the white boy; that the two white chiefs among them would take the boy and go in peace, or that the others would come and take him in war. Also, Chick-chick intimated that he must *klat-a-way.* The Indians made it plain that he was not going to *klat-a-way;* but looking abroad, they became more alarmed and excited by the cordon of whites about them.

"When the sun is so high," spoke Chick-chick, pointing, and using the sign language, "if we do not go forth with the boy, the white men will charge and kill all the Crows. One white boy is not worth that much."

After more excitement and talk, a youngish woman came, bearing a child in her arms, which was bawling and tear-stained—she vociferating wildly the time. Taking the unmusical youngster by the arm, the old chief stood him before Chick-chick. The boy was near nine years of age, the men judged, white beyond question, with long, golden hair braided, Indian fashion, down the sides of his head. He was neatly clothed in dressed buckskins, fringed and beaded, and not naked or half naked, as most Indian boys are in warm weather. It was not possible to tell what his face looked like in repose, for it was kneaded into grotesque lumps by his cries and wailing.

"He is a Crow; his skin is white, but his heart is Absaroke. It makes us bleed to see him go; our women will mourn all this snow for him, but to save my band I give him to you. Take him. He is yours."

Chick-chick lifted the child in his arms, where the small cause of all the turmoil struggled and pulled hair until he was forced to hold him out at arm's length. Mounting, they withdrew toward their friends. The council tepee fell in the dirt—a dozen squaws tugging at its voluminous folds. The small hostage was not many yards on his way toward his own kind before the Indian camp moved off toward the mountains, urging their horses with whip and lance. This movement was accelerated by a great discharging of white men's guns, who were supposed to be sacrificing the little white Crow to some unknown passions; whereas, they were merely celebrating the advent of the white child unharmed. He was indeed unharmed as to body, but his feelings had been torn to shreds. He added his small, shrill protesting yells to the general rejoicing.

Chick-chick, or Chickens, as the miners often called him, had not entered the expedition because of his love for children, or the color of this one in particular; so, at the suggestion of the chairman, it was turned over to a benevolent saloon-keeper, who had nine notches in his gun, and a woman with whom he abided. "Gold Nugget," as he was promptly named by the diggers and freighters, was supposed to need a woman, as it was adjudged that only such a one could induce him to turn off the hot water and cease his yells.

The cavalcade reached town, to find multitudes of dirt-begrimed men thronging the streets waiting for what sensation there was left in the affair. The infant had been overcome by his exertions and was silent. They sat him on the bar of his godfather's saloon, while the men shouldered their brawny way through the crowd to have a look at him—the lost white child in the Indian dress. Many drinks and pistol shots were offered up in his honor, and he having recovered somewhat, resumed his vocal protests. These plaints having silenced the crowd, it was suggested by one man who was able to restrain his enthusiasm, that the kid ought to be turned over to some woman before he roared his head off.

Acting on this suggestion, the saloon-keeper's female friend was given charge. Taking him to her little house back of the saloon, the child found milk and bread and feminine caresses to calm him until he slept. It was publicly proclaimed by the nine-notch saloon-keeper that the first man who passed the door of the kid's domicile would be number ten to his gun. This pronunciamiento insured much needed repose to Gold Nugget during the night.

In the morning he was partially recovered from fears and tears. The women patted his face, fed him to bursting, fingered the beautiful plaits of his yellow hair, and otherwise showed that they had not surrendered all their feminine sensibilities to their tumultuous lives.

They spoke to him in pleading voices, and he gurgled up his words of reply in the unknown tongue. The saloon-keeper's theory that it would be a good thing to set him up on the bar some more in order to keep trade, was voted both inhuman and impracticable by the women. Later in the day a young man managed to get on the young-ster's blind side, when by blandishments he beguiled him on to his pony in front of him. Thus he rode slowly through the streets, to the delight of the people, who responded to Gold Nugget's progress by volley and yell. This again frightened him, and he clung desperately to his new friend, who by waving his arm stilled the tempest of Virginia City's welcome, whereat the young man shouted, "Say—do you think this kid is runnin' for sheriff?"

The Gulch voted the newcomer the greatest thing that ever happened; took him into partnership, speculated on his previous career, and drank his health. Above all they drank his health. Unitedly they drank to his weird past—his interesting present, and to his future life and happiness, far into the night. It was good for business, said the saloon-keepers one to another.

On one of the same mountain winds which had heralded his coming was borne down the Gulch next morning the tragic words, "The kid has gone!"

"Gone?" said the miners; "gone whar?"

Alder promptly dropped its pick, buckled on its artillery, and assembled before the nine-notch man. "Where has the kid gone?" it demanded.

His woman stood beside the bar, wild-eyed and dishevelled. "I don't know, gentlemen—I don't have an idea. He was playing by the door of my shack last evening. I went in the house for a minute, and when I came out he was gone. I yelled, and men came, but we could not find him hide or hair."

"If any man has got that kid away from me—mind you this now—he will see me through the smoke," spoke nine-notch, as he rolled his eye malevolently for a possible reply.

Long search and inquiry failed to clear matters. The tracks around the house shed no new light. The men wound their way to their cabins up and down the Gulch, only answering inquiries by, "The kid is gone."

CHAPTER TWO

WHITE WEASEL

OR MANY DAYS THE ABSAROKE TROTTED AND bumped along, ceaselessly beating their ponies' sides with their heels, and lashing with their elk-horn whips. With their packs and travoix they could not move fast, but they made up for this by long hours of industrious ploding. An Indian is never struck without striking back, and his counter always comes when not expected. They wanted to manœuvre their women and children, so that many hills and broad valleys would lie between them and their vengeance when it should be taken. Through the deep cañons, among the dark pine trees, out across the bold table-lands, through the rivers of the mountains, wound the long cavalcade, making its way to the chosen valley of Crowland, where their warriors mustered in numbers to secure them from all thought of fear of the white men.

The braves burned for vengeance on the white fools who dug in the Gulch they were leaving behind, but the yellow-eyed people were all brothers. To strike the slaves of the gravel-pits would be to make trouble with the river-men, who brought up the powder and guns in boats every green-grass. The tribal policy was against such a rupture. The Crows, or Sparrowhawks as they called themselves, were already encompassed by their enemies, and only able by the most desperate endeavors to hold their own hunting-grounds against the Blackfeet, Sioux, and Cheyennes. Theirs was the pick and choosing of the northern plains. Neither too hot nor too cold, well watered and thickly grassed on the plains, swarming with buffalo, while in the winter they could retire to the upper valleys of the Big Horn River, where they were shut in by the impassable snow-clad mountains from foreign horse thieves, and where the nutritious salt-weed kept their ponies in condition. Like all good lands, they could only be held by a strong and brave people, who were made to fight constantly for what they held. The powder and guns could only be had from the white traders, so they made a virtue of necessity and held their hand.

Before many days the squaw Ba-cher-hish-a rode among the lodges with little White Weasel sitting behind her, dry-eyed and content.

Alder had lost Gold Nugget, but the Indians had White Weasel—so things were mended.

His foster-mother—the one from whom the chief had taken him— had stayed behind the retreating camp, stealing about unseen. She wore the wolfskin over her back, and in those days no one paid any attention to a wolf. In the dusk of evening she had lain near the shack where her boy was housed, and at the first opportunity she had seized him and fled. He did not cry out when her warning hiss struck native tones on his ear. Mounting her pony, she had gained the scouts, which lay back on the Indian trail. The hat-weavers (white men) should know White Weasel no more.

The old men Nah-kee and Umbas-a-hoos sat smoking over their talk in the purple shade of a tepee. Idly noting the affairs of camp, their eyes fell on groups of small urchins, which were scampering about engaging each other in mimic war. They shot blunt-headed arrows, while other tots returned the fire from the vantage of lariated ponies or friendly tepees. They further observed that little White Weasel, by his activity, fierce impulse, and mental excellence, was admittedly leading one of these diminutive war-parties. He had stripped off his small buckskin shirt, and the milk-white skin glared in the sunlight; one little braid had become undone and flowed in golden curls about his shoulders. In childish screams he urged his group to charge the other, and running forth he scattered all before his insistent assault.

"See, brother," spoke Nah-kee, "the little white Crow has been struck in the face by an arrow, but he does not stop."

"Umph—he will make a warrior," replied the other, his features relaxing into something approaching kindliness. The two old men understood what they saw even if they had never heard of the "Gothic self-abandonment" which was the inheritance of White Weasel. "He may be a war-chief—he leads the boys even now, before he is big enough to climb up the fore leg of a pony to get on its back. The arrow in his face did not stop him. These white men cannot endure pain as we do; they bleat like a deer under the knife. Do you remember the one we built the fire on three grasses ago over by the Big Muddy when Eash-dies split his head with a battleaxe to stop his noise? Brother, little White Weasel is a Crow."

A Crow

"It is so," pursued the other veteran; "these yellow-eyes are only fit to play badger in a gravel-pit or harness themselves to loaded boats, which pull powder and lead up the long river. They walk all one green-grass beside their long-horned buffalo, hauling their tepee wagons over the plains. If it were not for their medicine goods, we would drive them far away."

"Yes, brother, they are good for us. If we did not have their powder and guns, the Cut-Throats [Sioux] and the Cut-Arms [Cheyennes] would soon put the Absaroke fires out. We must step carefully and keep our eyes open lest the whites again see White Weasel; and if these half-Indian men about camp talk to the traders about him, we will have the camp soldiers beat them with sticks. The white traders would take our powder away from us unless we gave him to them."

"We could steal him again, brother."

"Yes, if they did not send him down the long river in a boat. Then he would go so far toward the morning that we should never pass our eyes over him again on this side of the Spiritland. We need him to fill the place of some warrior who will be struck by the enemy."

Seeing the squaw Ba-cher-hish-a passing, they called to her and said: "When there are any white men around the camps, paint the face of your little son White Weasel, and fill his hair with wood ashes. If you are careful to do this, the white men will not notice him; you will not have to part with him again."

"What you say is true," spoke the squaw, "but I cannot put black ashes in his eyes." She departed, nevertheless, glorious with the new thought.

Having fought each other with arrows until it no longer amused them, the foes of an idle hour ran away together down by the creek, where they disrobed by a process neatly described by the white men's drill regulations, which say a thing shall be done in "one time and two motions."

White Weasel was more complicated than his fellows by reason of one shirt, which he promptly skinned off. "See the white Crow," gurgled a small savage, as every eye turned to our hero. "He always has the war paint on his body. He is always painted like the big men when they go to strike the enemy—he is red all over. The war paint is in his skin."

"Now, let us be buffalo," spoke one, answered by others, "Yes, let us be buffalo." Accordingly, in true imitation of what to them was a familiar sight, they formed in line, White Weasel at the head as usual. Bending their bodies forward and swinging their heads, they followed down to the water, throwing themselves flat in the shallows. Now they were no longer buffalo, but merely small boys splashing about in the cool water, screaming incoherently and as nearly perfectly happy as nature ever intended human beings to be. After a few minutes of this, the humorist among them, the ultra-imaginative one, stood up pointing dramatically, and, simulating fear, yelled, "Here comes the bad water monster," whereat with shrill screams and much splashing the score of little imps ran ashore and sat down, grinning at their half-felt fear. The water monster was quite real to them. Who could say one might not appear and grab a laggard?

After this they ran skipping along the river bank, quite naked, as purposeless as birds, until they met two old squaws dipping water from the creek to carry home. With hue and cry they gathered about them, darting like quick-motioned wolves around worn-out buffalo. "They are buffalo, and we are wolves," chorussed the infant band; "bite them! Blind them! We are wolves! We will eat them!" They plucked at their garments and threw dirt over them in childish glee. The old women snarled at their persecutors and caught up sticks to defend themselves. It was beginning to look rather serious for the supposed buffalo, when a young warrior came riding down, his pony going silently in the soft dirt. Comprehending the situation, and being fairly among them, he dealt out a few well-considered cuts with his pony-whip, which changed the tune of those who had felt its contact. They all ran off, some holding on to their smarts— scattering away much as the wolves themselves might have done under such conditions.

Indian boys are very much like white boys in every respect, except that they are subject to no restraint, and carry their mischievousness to all bounds. Their ideas of play being founded on the ways of things about them, they are warriors, wild animals, horses, and the hunters, and the hunted by turns. Bands of these little Crows scarcely past toddling ranged the camp, keeping dogs, ponies, and women in a constant state of unrest. Occasional justice was meted out to them with a pony-whip, but in proportions much less than their deserts.

Being hungry, White Weasel plodded home to his mother's lodge, and finding a buffalo rib roasting near the fire he appropriated it. It was nearly as large as himself, and when he had satisfied his appetite, his face and hands were most appallingly greased. Seeing this, his mother wiped him off, but not as thoroughly as his condition called for, it must be admitted. Falling back on a buffalo robe, little Weasel soon fell into a deep slumber, during which a big dog belonging to the tent made play to complete the squaw's washing, by licking all the grease from his face and hands.

In due course he arose refreshed and ready for more mischief. The first opportunity which presented itself was the big dog, which was sleeping outside. "He is a young pony; I will break him to bear a man," said Weasel to himself. Straightway he threw himself on the pup, grasping firmly with heel and hand. The dog rose suddenly with a yell, and nipped one of Weasel's legs quite hard enough to bring his horse-breaking to a finish with an answering yell. The dog made off, followed by hissing imprecations from Ba-cher-hish-a, who rubbed the little round leg and crooned away his tears. He was not long depressed by the incident.

Now all small Indian boys have a regard for prairie dog or marmot's flesh, which is akin to the white boy's taste for candy balls and cream paste. In order to satisfy it the small Indian must lie out on the prairie for an hour under the broiling sun, and make a sure shot in the bargain. The white boy has only to acquire five cents, yet in the majority of cases that too is attended by almost overwhelming difficulties.

With three other boys White Weasel repaired to the adjoining dog-town, and having located from cover a fat old marmot whose hole was near the outskirts of the village, they each cut a tuft of grease-weed. Waiting until he had gone inside, they ran forward swiftly and threw themselves on the ground behind other dog mounds, putting up the grease-weed in front of themselves. With shrill chirping, all the marmots of this colony dived into their holes and gave the desert over to silence. After a long time marmots far away from them came out to protest against the intrusion. An old Indian warrior sitting on a nearby bluff, nursing morose thoughts, was almost charmed into good nature by the play of the infant hunters below him. He could remember when he had done this same thing—many, many grasses ago. More grasses than he could well remember.

The sun had drawn a long shadow before the fat marmot showed his head above the level of his intrenchments—his fearful little black eyes set and his ears straining. Three other pairs of black eyes and one pair of blue ones snapped at him from behind the grease-weed. There followed a long wait, after which the marmot jumped up on the dirt rim which surrounded his hole, and there waited until his patience gave out. With a sharp bark and a wiggling of his tail he rolled out along the plain, a small ball of dusty fur. To the intent gaze of the nine-year-olds he was much more important than can be explained from this viewpoint.

Having judged him sufficiently far from his base, the small hunters sprang to their knees, and drove their arrows with all the energy of soft young arms at the quarry. The marmot made a gallant race, but an unfortunate blunt-head caught him somewhere and bowled him over. Before he could recover, the boys were upon him, and his stage had passed.

Carrying the game and followed by his companions, Weasel took it home to his foster-mother, who set to skinning it, crooning as she did in the repeated sing-song of her race:

> My son is a little hunter,
> My son is a little hunter,
> Some day the buffalo will fear him,
> Some day the buffalo will fear him,
> Some day the buffalo will fear him,

and so on throughout the Indian list until the marmot was ready for cooking.

So ran the young life of the white Crow. While the sun shone, he chased over the country with his small fellows, shooting blunt arrows at anything living of which they were not afraid. No one corrected him; no one made him go to bed early; no one washed him but the nearby brook; no one bothered him with stories about good little boys; in fact, whether he was good or bad had never been indicated to him. He was as all Crow boys are—no better and no worse. He shared the affections of his foster-parents with several natural offspring, and shared in common, though the camp took a keen interest in so unusual a Crow. Being by nature bright and engaging, he foraged on every camp kettle, and made the men laugh as they lounged in the afternoon shade, by his absurd imitations of the war and scalp dances, which he served up seriously in his infant way.

Any white man could see at a glance that White Weasel was evolved from a race which, however remote from him, got its yellow hair, fair skin, and blue eyes amid the fjords, forests, rocks, and ice-floes of the north of Europe. The fierce sun of lower latitudes had burned no ancestor of Weasel's; their skins had been protected against cold blasts by the hides of animals. Their yellow hair was the same as the Arctic bear's, and their eyes the color of new ice. Little Weasel's fortunes had taken him far afield. He was born white, but he had a Crow heart, so the tribesmen persuaded themselves. They did not understand the laws of heredity. They had never hunted those.

CHAPTER THREE

The Coming of the Great Spirit

WITH THE YEARS WHITE WEASEL SPINDLED UP INTO A YOUTH whose legs quite naturally fitted around the barrel of a horse. He no longer had to climb up the fore leg of a camp-pony, but could spring on to those that ran in his father's herd and maintain his position there.

Having observed this, one night his foster-father said to him: "You are old enough, my son, to be trusted with my ponies out in the hills. You must begin to study the ponies, or you will never be able to take or hold any of your own. Not to have horses is not to hunt buffalo or go to the enemy, and not to have a wife. Go, then, when the morning comes, with your brother, and watch my herd. See that they feed safely; see that by evening they come to the lodges. You are old enough now to wear the loincloth; you must begin to be a man. You will never find your shadow-self here among the noisy lodges; it will only come to you out in the quiet of the hills. The Bad Spirits always have their arms out to clutch you when you are asleep in the night; as you ride in the shadows; when you ford the waters—they come in the wind, the rain, the snow; they point the bullet and the battleaxe to your breast, and they will warn the Sioux when you are coming after their ponies. But out in the hills the Sak-a-war-te will send some bird or some little wolf to you as his friend; in some way he will talk to you and give a sign that will protect you from the Bad Gods. Do not eat food or drink water; pray to him, and he will come to you; if he does not, you will be lost. You will never see the Spiritland when your body lies flat on the ground and your shadow has gone."

After saying this, his father's pipe died out, the mother put no more dry sticks on the fire, the shapes along the lodge walls died away in the gloom, and left the youth awake with a new existence playing through his brain. He was to begin to be a man. Already he had done in play, about the camp, the things which the warriors did among the thundering buffalo herds; he had imitated the fierce nervous effort to take the enemy's life in battle and the wolfish quest after ponies. He had begun to take notice of the great difference between himself and the girls about the camp; he had a meaning which they did not; his lot was in the field.

Before the sun rose he was one of the many noisy boys who ran about among the horses, trailing his lariat to throw over some pony which he knew. By a fortunate jerk he curled it about one's neck, the shy creature crouching under its embracing fold, knowing full well the awful strangle which followed opposition. With ears forward, the animal watched the naked youth, as he slowly approached him along the taut rope, saying softly; "Eh-ah-h-h—um-m-m-um-m-m—eh-h-h-h-h." Tying the rope on the horse's jaw, with a soft spring he fixed himself on its back, tucking his loincloth under him. Now he moved to the outskirts of the thronging horses, crying softly to them as he and his brother separated their father's stock from that of the neighbor herds. He had done this before, but he had never been responsible for the outcome.

The faint rose of the morning cut the trotting herd into dull shadowy forms against the gray grass, and said as plain as any words could to White Weasel: "I, the sun, will make the grass yellow as a new brass kettle from the traders. I will make the hot air dance along the plains, and I will chase every cloud out of the sky. See me come," said the sun to White Weasel.

"Come," thought the boy in reply, "I am a man." For all Indians talk intimately with all things in nature; everything has life; everything has to do with their own lives personally; and all nature can speak as well as any Crow.

Zigzagging behind the herd, they left the smell of smoke, carrion, and other nameless evils of men behind them, until the bark of wolf-dogs dulled, and was lost to their ears.

Daylight found the two boys sitting quietly, as they sped along beside the herd of many-colored ponies. To look at the white boy, with his vermilioned skin, and long, braided hair, one would expect to hear the craunch and grind of a procession of the war-cars of ancient Gaul coming over the nearest hill. He would have been the true part of any such sight.

"Brother," spoke his companion, "we must never shut our eyes. The Cut-Arms are everywhere; they come out of the sky, they come out of the ground to take our horses. You must watch the birds floating in the air; they will speak to you about the bad Indians, when you learn their talk; you must watch the wolves and the buffalo, and, above all, the antelope. These any one can understand. We must not let the ponies go near the broken land or the trees. The ponies themselves are fools, yet, if you will watch them, you will see them turn slowly away from an enemy, and often looking back, pointing with their ears. It may be only a bear which they go away from; for the ponies are fools—they are afraid of everything. The grass has been eaten off here by these buffalo, and the ponies wander. I will ride to the high hill, while you, brother, bring the herd slowly. Watch me, brother; I may give the sign of danger." Saying which, the older boy loped gracefully on ahead.

All day the herd grazed, or stood drooping, as the sun made its slow arc over the sky, while the boys sat on the ground in the shadows cast by their mounts, their eyes ceaselessly wandering. Many were the mysteries of horse-herding expounded by the one to the other. That the white Absaroke was hungry, it was explained, made no difference. Absarokes were often hungry out in the hills. The Dakotah were worse than the hunger, and to lose the ponies meant hunger in their father's lodge. This shadow-day herding was like good dreams; wait until the hail beat on the ponies' backs, and made them run before it; wait until the warriors fought about the camp, defending it; then it was hard work to hold them quietly. Even when the snow blew all ways at the same time, the Cut-Throats might come. White Weasel found a world of half-suspected things all coming to him at once, and gradually a realizing sense stole over him that the ponies and the eating and the land were very serious things, all put here for use and trouble to the Absaroke.

As the days wore on, the birds and the wild animals talked to the boy, and he understood. When they plainly hovered, or ran wildly, he helped to gather up the ponies and start them toward the lodges. If the mounted scouts came scurrying along the land, with the white dust in a long trail behind them, he headed for the cottonwoods with the herd, galloping. At times the number of the ponies in his charge changed, as his father won or lost at the game of "hand"; but after the dried-meat moon his father had brought home many new ponies from the camps of the Cut-Arms toward the Morning.

His father had often spoken praise of him beside the lodge-fire, and it made him feel good. He was beginning to be a man, and he was proud of it; he would be a warrior some day, and he would see that nothing hurtful happened to his father's horses.

It was now the month of the cold moon. The skies were leaden at times; the snow-laden winds swept down from the mountains, and in the morning Weasel's skin was blue and bloodless under his buffalo-robe when he started out for the hills, where the wind had swept the snow off from the weeds and grass. Never mind, the sun of the yellow grass had not cooked the ambition out of him, and he would fight off the arrows of the cold.

His brother, being older, had at last succumbed to his thirst for glory. He had gone with some other boys to try his fortune on other people's horses. Weasel was left alone with the herd. His father often helped him to take the ponies out to good grazing, and then left him. The Absaroke had been sore pressed by the Indians out on the plains, and had retired to the Chew-cârâ-âsh-Nitishic country, where the salt-weed grew. Here they could be pushed no farther. Aided by the circling wall of mountain, their own courage, and their fat horses, they could maintain themselves. Their scouts lay far out, and the camp felt as much security as a wild people can ever feel.

One day, as usual, Weasel had taken his ponies far away to fresh feed, that near the camps having been eaten off. The day was bright, but heavy, dense clouds drifted around the surrounding mountain-tops, and later they crawled slowly down their sides. Weasel noticed this as he sat shivering in his buffalo-robe; also he noticed far away other horse herds moving slowly toward the Arsha-Nitishic, along whose waters lay the camp of his people. He began to gather his ponies and rode circling about. They acted wildly—strung out and began to run. Glancing about, Weasel saw many big gray wolves loping along in unison with his charges.

It was not strange that wolves were in the vicinity of Indians. The wolves, the ravens, and the Indians were brothers in blood, and all followed the buffalo herds together. A lame or loose pony or a crippled Indian often went the way of the wolves, and many wolves' hides passed over the trader's counter. Thus they always got along together, with the raven last at the feast.

As Weasel turned his nervous eye about him, he knew that he had never seen so many wolves before. He had seen dozens and dozens, but not so many as these. They were coming in nearer to the horses—they were losing their fear. The horses were running—heads up, and blowing with loud snorts. Weasel's pony needed no whip; his dorsal action was swift and terrific.

The wolves did not seem to pay particular attention to him—they rather minded the herd. They gathered in great numbers at the head of the drove. Weasel could have veered off and out of the chase. He thought of this, but his blue eyes opened bravely and he rode along. A young colt, having lost its mother, ran out of the line of horses, uttering whinnies. Instantly a dozen gray forms covered its body, which sank with a shriek, as Weasel flashed by.

The leading ponies stopped suddenly and ran circling, turning their tails to the wolves, kicking and squealing viciously. The following ones closed up into the compact mass of horses, and Weasel rode, last of all, into the midst of them. What had been a line of rushing horses two arrow-flights long before, was now a closely packed mass of animals which could have been covered by a lariat. In the middle of the bunch sat Weasel, with his legs drawn up to avoid the crushing horses. It was all very strange; it had happened so quickly that he could not comprehend. He had never been told about this. Were

"In the middle of the bunch sat Weasel"

they really wolves, or spirits sent by the Bad Gods to destroy the boy and his horses?

All his waking hours had been spent with the ponies; he knew no other world; he had scarcely had any other thoughts. He was with them now, but instead of his protecting them they were protecting him. With their tails turned toward the circling mass of devil-animals, they struck and lashed when attacked. Nothing was heard but the snap of teeth, the stamp of hooves, the shrill squealing of horses, with an occasional thud followed by a yelp. The departing sun stole for a moment through a friendly rift in the clouds, encrimsoning the cold snow, and then departed, leaving the gray tragedy to the spirits of the night.

The smoke eddied from the top of the lodges; a bright spark showed from time to time as some one lifted an entrance flap; the ponies huddled in the dense bush; the dogs came out and barked at the wilderness of never ending plain. All was warmth and light, friendship, and safety—even the baying wolf-dogs were only defying the shades and distances out beyond for their own amusement; it was perfunctory.

"Why does not my son come in with the ponies?" asked the foster-father of his squaw, but she could only answer, "Why?"

Wrapping his robe about him, he walked to the edge of the camp and stood long squinting across the dusky land. He saw nothing to encourage him. Possibly the ponies had come in, but why not the boy?

Oh! That was possible! That had happened! A long walk failed to locate the horses. Then he spoke to a chief, and soon all was excitement.

"The little white Crow and his horses have not come in," was repeated in every lodge.

"The Sioux! The Sioux!" spoke the echo.

It was too dark for a search. "The Sioux" was the answer to every question, and no one hunted the Sioux by night. They might even now be on the outskirts. Swiftly the scouts made their way to the outposts. The warriors loaded their guns, and the women put out the fires. Every dog howled with all the energy of his emotional nature. There was no sleep for the Absaroke camp. It was seldom that an enemy got by the far-riding watchers of the Crow camps, but there was always a fear. It had happened.

Ba-chua-hish-a sobbed and wailed all night in her lodge, while the foster-father walked outside, speculating endlessly with his friends. Long before day he was mounted, and with a small party far on the way to the herd-grounds which he had chosen the day before.

As the plain began to unfold itself to their straining eyes, their quick ears ran ahead of them. A snarling, a horse-squealing, a curious medley of sounds, bore on them. Being old men, they knew. "It is the wolves," said they, almost in a chorus. Forward with a rush, a shrill yelling, and firing, swept the little party. The sun strove mightily to get over the mountains to help them. They now saw the solid mass of horses, with the wolves scurrying away on all sides. A faint answering human whoop came from the body of the beleaguered horse band. As the rescuers rode up, the ponies spread out from each other. Relieved from the pressure of the slimy fangs, the poor animals knew that men were better than wolves. Some of them were torn and bloody about the flanks; a few lay still on the snow with their tendons cut; but best of all which the Indians saw was little White Weasel sitting in the midst of the group. He allowed his robe to fall from his tight clutch. The men pushed their horses in among the disintegrating bunch. They saw that the boy's lips were without color, that his arms hung nerveless, but that his brave, deep eyes were open, and that they showed no emotion. He had passed the time of fear, and he had passed the time for hope, long hours ago.

They lifted him from his horse, and laid him on the ground, covered with many robes, while willing hands kneaded his marbled flesh. A fire was built beside him, and the old men marvelled and talked. It was the time when the gray wolves changed their hunting-grounds. Many had seen it before. When they sought the lower country, many grasses ago, to get away from the snow, one had known them to eat a Crow who happened in their way; this when he was a boy.

The wolves did not always act like this—not every snow. Sudden bad storms in the mountains had driven them out. The horse herds must be well looked after for a time, until the flood of wolves had passed down the valley.

The tired ponies stood about on the plain with their heads down. They, too, had become exhausted by the all-night fight. The sun came back, warm and clear, to see a more cheerful scene than it had left. Little Weasel spoke weakly to his father: "The Great Spirit came to me in the night, father—the cold wind whispered to me that White Weasel must always carry a hoof of the white stallion in his medicine-bag. 'It is the thing that will protect you,' said the wind. The white stallion lies over there—cut down behind. Kill him, and give me one of his rear hooves, father."

Accordingly, the noble beast, the leader of the horses in battle, was relieved of what was, at best, useless suffering—sacrificed to the gods of men, whom he dreaded less than the wolves—and his wolf-smashing hoof did useful things for many years afterward.

CHAPTER FOUR

CROOKED-BEAR

HITE WEASEL'S TOUGH BODY SOON recovered from the freezing night's battle between the animals. It had never been shielded from the elements, and was meat fed. The horses ate grass, because their stomachs were so formed, but he and the wolves ate meat. They had the canines. In justice to the wolves, it must be said that all three animals represented in the fight suffered in common; for if the boy had chilled veins, and the ponies torn flanks, many wolves were stiffened out on the prairie with broken ribs, smashed joints or jaws, to die of hunger. Nature brings no soup or warmth to the creature she finds helpless.

The boy's spiritual nature had been exalted by the knowledge that the Good God had not only held him in His saving arms during the long, cold, snarling night, but He had guaranteed his continual protection and ultimate salvation. That is no small thing to any person, but to the wild man, ever in close communion with the passing of the flesh, to be on intimate terms with the something more than human is a solace that dwellers in the quiescent towns are deadened to. The boy was not taught physical fear, but he was taught to stand in abject awe of things his people did not understand, and, in consequence, he felt afraid in strange places and at inopportune times.

One evening, as the family to which White Weasel belonged sat about the blaze of the split sticks in their lodge, Fire-Bear, the medicine-man, entered, and sat down to smoke his talk with the foster-father. Between the long puffs he said: "Crooked-Bear wants us to bring the white Absaroke to him. The hot winds have come down the valley, and the snow has gone, so we can go to the mountains the next sun. Will you go with me and take the boy? The Absaroke must do as the Crooked-Bear says, brother, or who knows what may happen to us? The old man of the mountain is strong."

After blinking and smoking for a time the foster-father said: "The boy's and Crooked-Bear's skins are of the same color; they are both Sparrowhawks in their hearts. His heart may be heavy out there alone in the mountains—he may want us to leave the boy by his fire. Ba-cher-hish-a would mourn if this were done. I fear to go, brother, but must if he ask it. We will be ready when the morning comes."

When the dark teeth of the eastern mountains bit into the gray of approaching day, the two old Indians and the boy were trotting along, one behind the other. The ponies slithered in the pools and little rivulets left by the melted snow, but again taking the slow, steady, mountainous, stiff-legged, swinging lope across the dry plain, they ate the flat miles up, as only those born on the desert know how to do.

The boy had often heard of the great Crow medicine-man up in the mountains near where the tribe hovered. He seldom came to their lodges, but the Indians frequently visited him. Weasel had never seen him, for the boys of the camp were not permitted to go near the sacred places where the old man was found. He had requested this of the chiefs, and the Absaroke children drank the mystery and fear of him with their mothers' milk. He was one of the tribal institutions, a matter of course; and while his body was denied them, his advice controlled in the council-lodges. His were the words from God.

Weasel was in the most tremendous frame of mind about this venture. He was divided between apprehension and acute curiosity. He had left his mother sobbing, and the drawn face of his father served only to tighten his nerves. Why should the great man want to see White Weasel, who was only a herd-boy? Was it because his hair and his eyes were not the color of other boys'? He was conscious of this difference. He knew the traders were often red and yellow like him, and not brown and black as the other people were. He did not understand the thing, however. No one had ever said he was anything else than an Absaroke; he did not feel otherwise.

Approaching the mountains, the travellers found the snow again, and climbed more slowly along the game-trails. They had blinded their path by following up a brook which made its way down a coulée. No one left the road to Crooked-Bear's den open to the prowling enemy. That was always understood. Hours of slow winding took them high up on the mountains, the snow growing deeper and less trodden by wild animals, until they were among the pines. Making their way over fallen logs, around jagged boulders, and through dense thickets, they suddenly dropped into a small wooded valley, then up to the foot of the towering terraces of bare rock, checkered with snow, where nothing came in winter, not even the bighorns.

Soon Weasel could smell fire, then dogs barked in the woods up in front. Fire-Bear called loudly in deep, harsh Indian tones, and was answered by a man. Going forward, they came first to the dogs—huge, bold creatures—bigger and different than any Weasel had ever seen. Then he made out the figure of a man, low in tone and softly massed against the snow, and beside him a cabin made of logs set against the rock wall.

This was Crooked-Bear. Weasel's mind had ceased to act; only his blue eyes opened in perfect circles, seemed awake in him, and they were fixed on the man. The big dogs approached him without barking— a bad sign with dogs. Weasel's mind did not concern itself with dogs. In response to strange words from the white medicine-man they drew away. Weasel sat on his pony while the older men dismounted and greeted Crooked-Bear. They did not shake hands—only "hat-wearers" did that. Why should an Indian warrior lose the use of his right hand for even an instant? His hand was only for his wife and children and his knife.

In response to the motion of his father's hand, the boy slid off his pony. Taking him by the shoulder, the father drew him slowly toward Crooked-Bear until they were directly in each other's presence. Weasel's eyes could open no farther. His whole training was that of an

Indian. He would not have betrayed his feelings under any circumstances; he was also a boy, and the occasion was to him so momentous that he was receiving impressions, not giving them. A great and abiding picture was fast etching itself on his brain; his spongelike child-mind drank up every drop of the weird situation.

He had seen a few white men in his life. He had not forgotten Virginia City, though terror had robbed him of his powers of observation during that ordeal. He had seen the traders at the post; he had seen the few white or half-white men who lived with his people, but they were not like this one.

The old man of the mountain was crooked as his name implied. He also suggested a bear. He looked rude even to the Indians. It seemed that Nature had laid her hands on his shoulder and telescoped him together. He was humpbacked. His arms and legs were as other men's are, though his shortened body made his hands fall to his knees.

He was dressed in Indian buckskin, greased to a shine and bronzed by smoke. He leaned on a long breech-loading rifle, and carried a huge knife and revolver in his belt. His hat was made of wolfskin after the Indian fashion, from underneath which fell long brown hair, carefully combed, in profuse masses. Seen closely he was not old—merely past middle life. His strong features were weather-stained and care-hardened. They were sculptured with many an insistent dig by Nature, the great artist; she had gouged deep under the brows; she had been lavish in the treatment of the nose; she had cut the tiger lines fearlessly, but she had covered the mouth and lost the lower face in a bush of beard. More closely, the whole face was open, the eyes mild, and all about it was reposeful—sad resolution dominated by a dome of brain. Weasel warmed under the gaze of the kind face—the eyes said nothing but good; they did more than that: they compelled him to step forward toward the strange figure, who put his hand on Weasel's shoulder and led him tenderly in the direction of the cabin door. Weasel had lost his fear and regained the use of his mind.

As the men stooped almost on hands and knees to enter the den of Crooked-Bear, they were greeted by the acrid smell of smouldering ashes, and probably by other odors native to their noses. Crooked-Bear stirred the ashes and laid split wood on them. It was pine which spat and broke out in a bright flame, painting the wild figures against the smoked logs and rock wall. It illumined a buffalo-covered bunk, piles of *parflèche* full of dried meat, a saddle and pack panniers, cooking pots and pans on the hearth, all deeply sooted, a table and chair made with an axe, and in one corner some shelves, equally rude, piled with brown and dirty books. Many small knick-knacks intruded their useful presence as one looked with more care, but the whole was the den of a man of some remote century. The sabre-toothed tiger might snarl at the door but for the Sharp's rifle standing in the corner; that alone made time and distance.

"Your ponies must starve tonight, brother," spoke Crooked-Bear. "Go put them in my house where the horses live in summertime. It is cold up here in the mountains—we have even no cottonwoods for them to eat. The bear and the wolves will not spring on them, though the big cats are about." All this said the white man in the language of the Absaroke, though it may be said it sounded strange in Weasel's ear. When he spoke to the dogs, the boy could not understand at all.

While the Indians looked after their ponies, the white man roasted meat and boiled coffee. On their return, seeing him cooking, Fire-Bear said: "Brother, you should have a squaw to do that. Why do you not take Be-Sha's daughter? She has the blood of the yellow-eyes in her. She would make your fire burn."

"Tut, tut," he replied, "no woman would make my fire burn. My fire has gone out." With a low laugh, Crooked-Bear added, "No woman would stay long up here, brothers; she would soon run away." Fire-Bear said nothing, for he did not understand. He himself would follow and beat the woman and make her come back, but he did not say so.

Having eaten, and passed the pipe, Fire-Bear asked the hermit how the winter was passing—how the dry meat was lasting—what fortune had he in hunting, and had any enemies beset him? He was assured his good friends, the Absaroke, had brought him enough dry meat, after the last fall hunt, to last him until he should no longer need it. The elk were below him, but plentiful, and his big dogs were able to haul enough up the hills on his sleds. He only feared for his tobacco, coffee, and ammunition; that had always to be husbanded, being difficult to get and far to carry. Further, he asked his friend, the Indian, to take some rawhides back to the women, to be dressed and made into clothes for his use.

"Has my brother any more talking papers from the yellow-eyes? Do the white men mean to take the Sioux lands away from them? The Sioux asked the Absaroke last fall to help drive the white men out of the country, saying, 'If they take our lands to dig their badger-holes in, they will soon want yours.' The Absaroke would not help the Cut-Throats; for they are dogs—they wag their tails before they bite," spoke Fire-Bear.

"Yes, brother," replied Crooked-Bear; "if you should, by aiding the Sioux, get rid of the white men, and even this you would not be able to do—you would still have the Sioux, who are dogs, always ready to bite you. No, brother, have nothing to do with them, as I have counselled you. The Sak-a-war-te said this to me: 'Before the grass on the plains shoots, send a strong, fat-horse war-party to the enemy and strike hard. Sweep their ponies away—they will be full of sticks and bark, not able to carry their warriors that moon; tear their lodges down and put their fires out; make their warriors sit shivering in the plum bushes. That is the way for the Crows to have peace.' The Great Spirit has said to me: 'Tell the Absaroke that they can never run the buffalo on the plains in peace, until the Chis-chis-chash, the Dakotahs, and the Piegan dare not look them in the face. That, and that only, is the path.'"

Far into the night the men talked of the tribal policy—it was diminutive statesmanship, commercial politics with buffalo meat for money. As Crooked-Bear sat on his hewn chair, he called the boy to him, put his arm around him, and stood him against his knee. The youth's head rose above the rugged face of the master of Indian mystery; he was in his first youth, his slender bones had lengthened suddenly in the last few years, and the muscles had tried hard to catch up with them. They had no time to do more than that, consequently Weasel was more beautiful than he would ever be again. The long lines of grace showed under the tight buckskins, and his face surveyed the old man with boyish wonder. Who can know what the elder thought of him in return? Doubtless he dreamed of the infinite possibilities of so fine a youth. He

"He called the boy to him and put his arm around him"

whose fire had gone out mused pleasantly as he long regarded the form in whom they were newly lighted.

Slowly he began to speak, using the Indian forms of speech, and supplementing them with the gestures which only Indians can command. "Brother, we have lived a long time. We have made the medicine strong for the Absaroke. We have taken the words of the Good Gods to the council-lodge when the tribe ran wildly and knew not which way to turn. We will follow soon the others who have gone to the Shadow-land. The Absaroke will be left behind, and they must have wise men to guide them when we are gone. This young man will be one of those—I have seen that in my dreams. He must stay here with me in the lonely mountains, and I will teach him the great mystery of the white men, together with that of the people of his own tribe. He will visit his father's lodge whenever his heart is hungry. He owes it to himself and to his people to grow strong in the mystery, and then some day the tribe will lean on him. Shall he stay, brothers?"

White Weasel, with arms dropped to his side, made no move. The flame from the hearth lighted one of his starlike eyes as it stood open, regardful of the strange old man. The Indians passed the pipe, and for a long time there was no sound save the snapping of the fire and the pines outside popping with the cold.

At last Fire-Bear spoke: "We have had our ears open, brother. Your talk is good. The Sak-a-war-te demands this. The boy shall stay."

Weasel's foster-father held his peace. His was the sacrifice, but the Great Spirit could not ask too much of him. In reply to another inquiry, he said that the boy should stay; then wrapping himself in his robe, he lay down before the fire to hide his weakness.

"Will you stay with me?" asked the Wonder-Worker of the boy, stroking his yellow hair and pouring the benevolence of his fire-lighted face in a steady stream on the youth.

"You have no ponies to herd, father. What shall I do?" he asked.

"I have no ponies for you to herd, but I have many mysteries here," tapping the boy's forehead with his finger, "for you to gather up and feed on, and they are greater than ponies."

"I will stay, father."

CHAPTER FIVE

THE WHITE MEDICINE

THAT THE SUN ROSE WITH CUSTOMARY PRECISION MADE LITTLE difference to the sleepers in the mountain den. Little of its light crept down the hole against the rock wall, and none of it penetrated the warm buffalo-robes. The dogs, growing uneasy, walked about and scratched at the door; they had not been disturbed by last night's vigil. Waking, one by one, the men threw off the robes and went out; all but the boy, who lay quite still, his vitality engaged in feeding the growing bones and stretching muscles.

Out by the stable Crooked-Bear said: "Take your ponies and that of the boy and ride away. They will starve here, and you must go before they weaken and are unable to carry you. A boy changes his mind very quickly, and he may not think in the sunlight what he did in the fire-light. I will be kind to him. Tell Ba-cher-hish-a that her son will be a great chief in a few grasses."

Silently, as only the cats and the wolves and the Indians conduct themselves, the men with the led horses lost themselves among the trees, leaving Crooked-Bear standing by his abode with the two great cross-bred mastiffs, on their hind legs, leaning on him and trying to lick his face. As they stood together, the dogs were taller than he, and all three of them about the same color. It was a fantastic scene; a few goblins, hoarse mystery birds, Indian devils, and what not beside, might have been added to the group and without adding to its strangeness. Weasel had found a most unearthly home; but as he awoke and lay looking about the cabin, it did not seem so awfully strange. Down through the ages—borne through hundreds of wombs—in some mysterious alcove of the boy's brain had survived something which did not make the long-haired white man working about the fire, the massive dogs, the skins of wild animals, the sooty interior, look so strange.

As Weasel rose to a sitting posture on the bunk, the dogs got up also. "Down with you! Down with you, Eric! And you, Hope! You must not bother the boy," came the hermit's words of command. The dogs understood, and lay heavily down, but their eyes shone through heavy red settings as they regarded the boy with unarrested attention.

"I am afraid of your dogs, father; they are as big as ponies. Will they eat me?"

"No; do not be afraid. Before the sun goes over the mountains they will eat any one who would raise his hand against you. Come, put your hand on their heads. The Indians do not do this; but these are white dogs, and they will not bite any one who can put his hand on their heads," spoke Crooked-Bear in his labored way with the Indian tongue. He had never mastered all the clicks and clucks of it.

The meat being done, it was put on the table, and White Weasel was persuaded to undertake his first development. The hermit knew that the mind never waits on a starved belly, so he explained to the boy that only dogs ate on the ground. That was not obvious to the youngster; but he sat in the chair and mauled his piece of meat, which was in a tin plate. He drank his coffee out of a tin cup, which he could see was full better than a hollow buffalo horn, besides having the extra blandishment of sugar in it. As the hermit, occupying an upturned pack-saddle opposite, regarded the boy, he could see that Weasel had a full forehead—that it was not pinched like an Indian's; he understood the deep, wide-open eyes which were the color of new ice, and the straight, solemn nose appealed to him also. The face was formal even to the statuesque, which is an easy way of saying he was good-looking. The bearer of these messages from his ancestors to Crooked-Bear quite satisfied him. He knew that the baby Weasel had been forcibly made to enter a life from which he himself had in mature years voluntarily fled, and for which neither was intended. They had entered from opposite doors only, and he did not wish to go out again, but the boy might. He determined to show him the way to undo the latching.

After breakfast began the slow second lesson of the white man's mystery. It was in the shape of some squaw's work, and again the boy thought unutterable protests. Crooked-Bear had killed an elk the day before, some considerable distance down the mountain, and taking his dogs with the sledges, they sallied down to get it. What with helping to push the heavy loads in aid of the dogs and his disgust of being on foot, at their noon homecoming White Weasel's interest began to flag.

Crooked-Bear noticed this, and put even more sugar into the boy's coffee. He had a way of voicing half-uttered thoughts to himself, using his native tongue, also repeating these thoughts as though to reënforce them. "I must go slow—I must go slow, or the boy will balk. I must lead him with a silken thread; the rawhide will not do—it will not do." Meanwhile the growing youth passed naturally into oblivion on the bunk.

"These Indians are an indolent people," the prophet continued. "They work only by fits and starts, but so am I indolent too. It befits our savage way of life," saying which, he put some coffee-berries into a sack and began pounding them with an axe. "I do not know—I do not remember to have been lazy; it does not matter now if I am. No one cares, and certainly I do not. I have tramped these mountains in all weathers; I have undergone all manner of hardships, yet they said I could not be a soldier in the armies down south. Of course not—of course not; a humpback could not be a soldier. He is fit only to swear at. Men would laugh at a crooked-back soldier. *She* could see nothing but my back. Ah—ah—it is past now. Men and women are not here to see my back; the trees and the clouds, the mountains and my dogs, do not look at my spine. The Indians say my back was bent by my heavy thoughts. The boy there has a straight back, and I hope he may walk among men. I will see that he does; I will give him the happiness which was denied me, and it pleases me to think that I can do this. I will create a happiness which the vicissitudes of this strange life seem to have denied him, saying, 'Weasel, you are to be a starved and naked nomad of the plains.' No! No! Boy; you are not to be a starved and naked nomad of the plains. I have in my life done no intentional evil, and also I have done no intentional good; now this problem of the boy has come to me—how it reaches out its roots for the nourishing things and how its branches spread for the storms!"

Having accompanied these thoughts by the beating of the axe, the hermit arose, and stood gazing on the sleeping lad. "Oh, if I had only had your back! Oh! Oh! Oh! But if only you had had my opportunities and education—well, I am not a god; I am only a man; I will do what a man can."

When the boy awoke, the hermit said, "My son, did you ever make a gun speak?"

"No; my father's gun hangs with his mystery-bag on his reclining-mat, and a woman or child dare not lay their fingers on it."

"Would you like to make a gun talk?" came gently, but Weasel could only murmur. The new and great things of life were coming fast to him. He would almost have given his life to shoot a gun; to own one was like the creation, and the few similar thoughts of men; it was beyond the stars.

"Weasel," said the man, taking up a carbine, and calling him by name—which is un-Indian—"here is a gun; it loads in the middle; I give it to you; it is yours." With which he handed the weapon to the boy.

After some hesitation Weasel took the gun, holding it stiffly in front of him, as an altar boy might a sacred thing. He could say nothing, and soon sat down, still holding the firearm, regarding it for a long time. When he could finally believe he was not dreaming, when he comprehended that he really did own a gun, he passed into an unutterable peace, akin to nothing but a mother and her new-born child. His white father stepped majestically from the earth that Weasel knew into the rolling clouds of the unthought places.

"Tomorrow I will take my gun, and you will take your gun, and we will walk the hills together. Whatever we see, be it man or beast, your gun may speak first," proposed the prophet.

"Yes, father, we will go out with the coming of the sun. My heart is as big as the mountains; only yesterday I was a herd-boy, now I own a gun. This brought it all to me," the boy said almost to himself, as he fumbled a small bag hanging at his neck. The bag contained the dried horse's hoof.

Throwing back his long hair, the prophet fixed his face on his new intellectual garden. He saw the weeds, and he hardly dared to pull them, fearing to disturb the tender seeds which he had so lately planted. Carefully he plucked at them. "No, my son, that was not your medicine which brought the gun, but my medicine; the medicine of the white man brought it to you. The medicine of the white man brought the gun to you because the Great Spirit knew you were a white boy. The medicine of the white man is not carried in a buckskin bag; it is carried here." And the prophet laid his finger on his own rather imposing brow; he swept his hair away from it with a graceful gesture, and smiling on the youth, he waited to see whether the seed had come up with the bad weed.

Weasel's hand left the bag, and followed down to the gun while he looked at his master. It might be so; no Indian boy whom he knew had ever had a gun. This firearm absorbed him, and the man felt it would continue to do so for some time to come; therefore he said no more.

Bright and early was the start of the hunters in the morning. They left the dogs in the cabin, and with snowshoes slung to their backs, followed down the sledge-trail toward the bare foothills, where the game was. In and out among the shadows of the pine trees passed the figures, vigorous with the mountain ozone, and both happy in their respective ways. On reaching a proper place, they adjusted the broad, oval rackets, and skirted along the timber-line, watching the hills below them, from which the wind had blown the snow. It was not difficult to find game in those days, before the coming of the white men bearing their long-range rifles. Far out on the plain their trained eyes saw the bands of antelope, and, nearer, herds of mule-deer working about in the ravines. "But," said the boy, "my first shot must be at an elk or a bighorn, father."

"Come then, my son, we will go round this point of the hill, and on the sunny southern slope we will find the elk—great bands of them. You shall shoot one, and when you have done that, the herd-boy will be a hunter."

As had been predicted, in due course of their walk they beheld bands of elk lying about or walking slowly, their yellow backs gleaming in the morning sun. The warm winds from the valleys were coming up toward the arctic mountaintops and away from the elk. "Take off your snowshoes, my son; they creak on the snow—the elk will hear them; we must go down this ravine, and when we are near enough, you will shoot."

Under cover of the rocks and sparse pines they slowly made their well-considered way noiselessly, the boy's eyes blazing with the hunter's lust, and the old man watching him eagerly. From time to time the Weasel lifted his head above the rim-rock of the ravine to note the position of their approach, but the hermit's heedful eye bore only on his pupil. They had worked their way, after the hunter manner, a long distance downward, and hoped soon to be in a position for a safe shot. The cañon-like ravine which they were following narrowed suddenly; the snow lay in deep drifts against its sides, making it necessary for them to go slowly along the ledges of the rim-rock, the boy always first. As they were about to round the point where the coulée tightened, a big yellow form drifted like a windblown feather on to them; it suddenly appeared not twenty feet from their faces, and it was a mountain-lion. Both the men and the animal stopped, the men straightening up while the cougar crouched down. The cat bared its fangs, the boy raised his carbine; both were in search of game, but neither for what he had found. The gun reached its place; the coulée echoed with the heavy report, and through the enveloping smoke flew the great cat as though also impelled by gunpowder. The boy had not missed his mark, and the lion his only by a small margin. The steep snowdrift yielded under his frantic claws, carrying him many yards down the sides.

"Load your gun and shoot him, Weasel; I shall not shoot," came the hermit's voice. The position of his long rifle belied his words, but the youth did not look behind. He fumbled for a cartridge, was slow in working the strange mechanism of the arm, but he was ready by the time the cat, much frustrated by the unresisting snow, had nearly reached him. Again the cañon chorussed to the rifle, and as the heavy black powder-smoke drifted off on the friendly wind, the boy saw that he had killed. All had happened too quickly for his brain if not for his arm.

"Load your gun," came the voice of command in English. The tense situation made the new language strike Weasel's brain through his ear as his bullet had struck the monster. The sound of it was what conveyed the meaning, and the harsh bang of the words went home. An Indian would have had to gluck and cluck and glut for half a minute to make these three words plain. It would have sounded more like grace before meat than a command.

Weasel again broke his rifle and shoved the brass shell home, never looking elsewhere than at the yellow spot of fur on the white snow below him, as its fierce electric nerves slowly softened its expiring motions into quiet. He had never had even a dream of victory such as had taken form before him. He had known old Indian hunters who rode on a lion's skin in the ceremonial days, and he knew what warriors in the tribe wore the grizzly bear-claw necklaces—every one knew those men. Could it be that he would ride on a lion's skin? Could it be that he would carry a gun which loaded in the middle? Yes, it could be if he only had a horse, but ponies were easier than guns or lions' skins in the Indian world. What a vista of power and glory opened in the boy's mind! What vanity of his could not yet be satisfied?

The hermit glanced over the rim-rock and saw the elk in long lines trotting away; he could hear the joints cracking, but his cabin was full of meat. "Boy, this was a white man's medicine-hunt. Could any Indian do that for you?" But the boy heeded not; with a series of wolfish yells he slid down the snowy incline toward his fallen foe. The hermit followed, and drawing their knives, they raised the hide while the body was yet warm, taking head and tail and claws. Weasel was delirious with joy; he laughed and jabbered and ki-yied, while the pleased old man calculated that he had reduced the boy to a state of mind when it was safe to burden his wild young charge with something quite as serious for him as tigers' skins. He would make him begin his English.

They made their way back to the snowshoes—back to the sledge-road—up to the cabin—received a welcome from the dogs; but the coffee had less sugar than before. Economy was a watchword with him who trailed his necessities over the long journey from the traders on pack-ponies, and so the lion skin tacked on the wall was enough for the boy.

Gradually the man brought English words into the play of conversation, and Weasel sought the key to the white medicine which had so exalted him. The nouns came first, and he soon began to piece them out with other parts of speech; his ear accustomed itself, and with it all came new and larger thoughts carefully strewn in his way by the prophet.

They hunted together; did the little healthy work found in their simple manner of life which no longer seemed fitted for women only; and the grave old man at last saw the spark which he had lighted burst into flame. It was the warmth of human kindness which is the base of everything ennobling to man.

One day when the buds of the leaves were beginning to show themselves, in response to nature's inviting smiles, the dogs barked furiously. The two dwellers of the cabin seized their rifles, ran out to places which had been selected by them for their strategic advantages in calm moments, and waited. Before long they heard challenges in the well-known Absaroke, which they answered.

"Do not talk English to your people, my son; they will not understand," said the hermit; but what he feared was their suspicion of the transformation of the lad. The Absaroke, no more than the Dakotahs, understood or loved the white man; they merely tolerated him for tribal reasons. The prophet had ingratiated himself by fortunate circumstances and an abounding tact.

The newcomers were a dozen chiefs of the tribe, the boy's Indian father among them. They drove a few led ponies belonging to Crooked-Bear, which they were returning after their wintering with the Absaroke herds. The quickly shooting mountain grasses would support them at this season.

Long and seemingly interminable talks followed the pipe about the prophet's blazing hearth. He filled their minds with strong, sensible advice, reënforcing it by supposed inspired sources, until the tobacco which he had appropriated for such occasions gave out. It was a cheap and in fact the only way by which he could purchase immunity from violence—a safe wintering for his ponies and his fall supply of dried buffalo meat.

His influence was boundless, and while he hoped quite as much as the Indians that the white men would never come to these parts during his lifetime, he also knew that they would. He heard reports that the miners were invading the Sioux territory from the south; he knew gold, and he knew white men, and he realized what the combination always produced. In this strait he saw that the efforts of the Sioux would be so taxed to oppose the progress that the Absaroke would profit by their preoccupation. His revelations always favored the alliance between the Absaroke and the yellow-eyes. No one can ever know how much this forgotten hermit of the Chew-cârâ-âsh-Nitishic did for his race in the days when the Indians of the northern plains made their last stand before the white men. The Indians from King Philip's time never understood the powers, resources, and numbers of the white people. Even the Crows in those days wavered before the boastful envoys of the neighbor tribes. The Indians had hunted out of the country the Metis, the Pea-Soups, or the French half-breeds, together with the white trappers, who had often contracted Indian marriages, and who had followed the fortunes of the early fur trade.

At that time old frontiersmen like Norris, who had for years followed up and down the plains, and across the range, admitted that a strong party of seasoned trappers was not safe east of the Big Horn Mountains.

The long palaver terminated with the Indians' promise to send out war-parties against the other tribes. The Weasel was not able to resist a very natural desire to go again to the camps, to visit his foster-mother, the boys of his childhood, and deeper yet to bear the gun and the lion's skin. The important men of the visiting party had come to regard White Weasel with some sort of veneration; he had that about him which was not quite understandable; he was supposed to be near the unknown Power.

CHAPTER SIX

JOHN ERMINE

FOR A FEW DAYS AFTER THE DEPARTURE OF THE BOY THE HERMIT felt depressed; he had added a human interest to his life, which previously had been satisfied by communion with nature alone. The bugs, the plants, the birds, the beasts, the dogs, the hunting, had sufficed. The seat on the rock wall above the cabin, where he mused, and where his eyes went forward over interminable miles of cloud-flecked plain and tier after tier of ragged mountain ranges, had satisfied him, while his mind wandered backward among the years before he became a hermit.

But shortly the time arrived when he was compelled to make his semiannual trip with his packhorses to the traders for his supplies of ammunition, of pots and pans, of tobacco, blankets, and foodstuffs, without which he could not exist. This journey was always tedious, hard, and dangerous; but he tried always to do it while the horses of the enemy out on the plains were thin and as yet unserviceable. With all the circumspection he was able to use, he had on several occasions nearly lost his life; but needs must, he could renounce everything on earth except his belly. However, this time he accomplished his journey, and aside from straying ponies, turning packs, with the other inevitables of desert life, he, safe and well provided, found his cabin again. The Indians had told him that White Weasel had gone with a war-party. That was nothing; all men in the wild country were more or less at war all the time. "I hope the boy keeps that corn-silk on his head," soliloquized the hermit; "also I think it would be a good thing for the young savage if he is forced to leave other people's alone. A fresh scalp in that boy's hand will make an extra year's work for me. It cannot be helped—it cannot be helped; it is the law of nature, only that law operates badly out here. What does it matter, however? The women can correct the loss of a man more or less in the world."

With the return of spring came the elk and big-horn. They walked into his park and blew their whistles as they smelled the odors from his hearth. The big gray bears came out of their winter caves and rumbled past his door. These were his greatest foes, constantly stampeding his ponies, even clawing at his heavy log horse-barn, where he always kept one horse to hunt the others with, and trying to circumvent his meat-arbor—a device hung on a pole high up between two slender trees, which was operated up and down by a rawhide rope. Small black bears often put this out of action, but the dogs were usually able to chase these away. Not so with the silver-tips; for at times one of the playful brutes would come round to indulge himself in the sport of chasing Eric and Hope about the dooryard over their own preserves. They both had been slashed and hugged at intervals in their youth, and so took the big bears at their own estimate. The long, fifty-caliber rifle was called upon on such occasions, and thus far with success.

One day, at the beginning of summer, the boy returned to the hermit's nest—was barked at, challenged, and finally greeted.

"Have you blinded your ponies' trail carefully, coming up from the valley? The enemy is abroad in the land these days," was asked and answered satisfactorily. The boy's features, which were rather grave in response to the seriousness of his life, were relaxed and beaming. There was an eagle feather in his hair, hanging down behind. He led the pony loaned by the prophet, which bore a bunch of buckskins, and was mounted on a fine animal, quite in the warrior class, with a new elkhorn saddle. His panther skin was rolled behind him. Dismounting, he carefully undid this, and from its folds drew forth a scalp—a braid of long hair, the skin stretched on a wooden ring and half covered down the plat with silver disks made of pounded silver dollars.

"It was a Dakotah, father, and I put his fire out with the medicine gun you gave me. I have danced it with the warriors; I am a warrior now."

The old man's worst fears had been realized, but after eating he had the story from White Weasel.

"When I reached the village, my father's and mother's hearts grew big at the sight of my gun and lion's skin. My mother had made the buckskins you sent down by my father into clothes both for yourself and for myself." Here he presented the hermit with his new dress, made beautiful with yellow ochre and with long fringes at back and sleeves, and open at the front, as was the white man's custom.

"Long-Horse," the boy continued, "was making up a party to go to the Dakotahs. I asked to be one of them, but he thought I was young. I said my medicine was strong and that my horse was fat. He said I was young to learn the warpath secret, but after smoking my talk he consented. I had only eight cartridges and one horse, all the other Indians having two apiece. Your old pack-pony is a war-horse now, father; he has carried a warrior," and the turquoise eyes gleamed brilliantly. "Long-Horse had a big band; we made the warpath medicine and travelled many sleeps with our backs to the sun. One morning our scouts found two men, an Absaroke and a white man, and brought them in. They belonged to the white warriors' camp, which was fighting the Dakotahs, who were all around them, and these men were going for help. Long-Horse moved toward this place guided by the men we had met. Before the sun was up, the Absaroke rode into the camp of the white soldiers, and they were glad to see us. They had the white cloth lodges and many wagons, but their horses had been taken by the Dakotahs and they had lost some soldiers. The white men had put their dead men in the ground. I saw where they had dug in the earth and left mounds such as the prairie dog builds. The camp was on the low ground, and back of this were bluffs. When the sun gave light, we could see the Cut-Throats swarm on their hill as the ants do when you lift a stone. There were five Cut-Throats to one white soldier, and the white men could not go out to them. While the white men had no women, they had more wagons than I could count, loaded with sugar and coffee until the wheels cut the ground. I never knew there was so much coffee and sugar; where does it come from, father? The white men are rich, and there are so few of them that each has more than he wants. In a place of that kind the Absaroke would have run away, but the white men cannot run, and they think more of the coffee and sugar than they do of their own lives. It made my head weak when I saw the enemy; they rode swiftly; they were all warriors, for they all had the war-feathers in their hair. They had guns, and as they rode they made the gestures of women and snakes and dogs at us. They rode away from a spot which they pointed at, and then they pointed at us, saying we were buffalo that always ran away like this. Long-Horse and the white chief, a big man with short hair, made a long talk. The Absaroke gave their old travelling-ponies to the white warriors, who put their own saddles on them. These white soldiers mounted the ponies on the wrong side, and tired as the horses were, they jumped like rabbits under them. Though I was afraid of the enemy, I had to laugh, father.

"When we were ready, we charged the enemy, and they fled before us; we followed them until they gained the rough hills. We fired at the Dakotahs, and they fired at us, they always working backward in the rough cañons, where we were afraid to follow on horseback because Long-Horse said they were trying to lead us into an ambuscade. All day we fought, although very few were killed. At night the white soldiers and many Absaroke rode swiftly back to the camp. Long-Horse with half of the Absaroke stopped in the strong woods high up on one side of a ravine, and I stayed with them. I had only four cartridges left. All night we lay there and allowed their scouts to go down the cañon without firing on them. In the early morning we heard the Dakotahs coming; they rode down the cut before our faces, not knowing we were there. When Long-Horse gave his war-whoop, we all fired, and jumping on our ponies charged into them. The ground was covered with dying horses and men. My heart grew big, father; everything before my eyes swam red, and I do not remember much except that I rode behind a big Dakotah and shot him in the back. He fell from his horse to the ground and tried to gain his feet, but I rode the pack-pony over him, knocking him down so that he lay still. I turned round and shot him again before he died, and then I took his hair. He had a beautiful head-dress of feathers, which I took, but I left his gun, for it was heavy and a poor one. I chased his pony, the fine war-horse which is out in the stable. The Dakotahs who were not killed had all run away, so I ran the dead man's pony back to camp, where with the help of other Indians I caught him. Long-Horse was killed, and a few Absaroke wounded, but we got many scalps, one of which is mine.

"The white soldiers took me to their lodge and gave me coffee which was heavy with sugar. They spoke your language to me, but I could not understand much of it. A half-Indian man talked the Absaroke for me in their tongue, and when I said I was a Crow—for that is what the white men call us—they laughed until my heart grew bad. They asked me if there were any more Crows whose hair was the color of the dry grass, and then they continued to laugh. They said I must have been born on a frosty morning. I did not know what to say, but I saw their hearts warmed to me, and I did nothing. They gave me cartridges, blankets, sugar, and coffee, until the old pack-pony could carry no more. The big chief of the white men wanted me to stay with him, and promised to give me anything I wanted from the wagons. He talked long with the warriors, asking them to leave me with him, and the Absaroke said he could have me, but I did not want to stay. At one time I thought the white soldiers were going to make me stay, for they took me on their shoulders and carried me about the camp, laughing and yelling. I was afraid. Those men were bigger than Indians, and, father, their arms were as hard and strong as the gray bear's. They were always laughing; they roared like the buffalo bulls.

"My color is the same as theirs, father; many of them had hair like mine, though they cut it short. I am a Crow, but I do not understand these things." Whereat the boy fell into a deep meditation.

Cautiously the hermit approached. "Your heart warms to the white man, does it not, my son?"

"Yes, all white men are good to me; they give me everything I want; they are rich, and their hearts are big. They do not know how to keep their horses; they are fools about them, and they mount from the wrong side. I never heard a white man speak to a horse in that camp. When they walk up to a pony, the pony does not know whether they come as a friend or an enemy. Some day I am going to Ashar-Ra, where the white soldiers live. They told me that when I came they would load my pony down with gifts. But I must first learn to talk as you do, father."

Here, at last, was light to brighten the hopes of the hermit. The boy's ambition had been aroused. What if he had gone to war, and what if he did have the much-treasured scalp in his possession? He had only followed the hermit's advice to his tribe concerning war. Then, too, the old man had picked up newspapers at the traders' which told of the invasion of the Black Hills by the white miners. He knew this would provoke war with the Sioux, and it occurred to him that the best possible way to introduce White Weasel to his own people would be through contact with the army. He could go with them, and they might reclaim him. He could not possibly go through the industrial institutions, but he must speak English. There was plenty of time for that, since he could kill elk within a mile of his door with which to maintain himself. He would begin.

"Yes, you must work hard with me now to speak as the white men do. You will soon be a man; you are no longer a boy. You are a white man, but you were brought up by the Absaroke, and you will go back to your own people some day. The more you see them, the better you will like them."

"Why must I go to the white people, father? You do not go to them, and you are a white man."

The hunchback hermit leaned with his head on his hands for a long time; he had not foreseen this. Finally, "You will go because they are your own people; you will join them when they fight the Sioux. You think there are not many of them. Weasel, I am not a liar, and I say there are more white men on the earth than there are buffalo. You are young, you are brave, and you are straight in the back; their hearts will warm toward you. You will grow to be a white chief and own many wagons of coffee and sugar. Some day, Weasel, you will want a white woman for a wife. You have never seen a white woman; they are not like these red squaws; they are as beautiful as the morning, and some day one of them will build a fire in your heart which nothing but death can put out.

"From now on I shall no longer call you White Weasel, but will give you a white name which you must answer to. There shall be no Indian mystery about it, and you shall bear it all your life. I will call you"—and here the hermit again relapsed into thought.

"I will call you John Ermine; that is a good strong white name, and when you are asked what it is, do not say White Weasel—say, 'My name is John Ermine.' Now say it!" And the young man ran the thing over his tongue like a treble drag on a snare-drum.

"Now again, after me: 'My—name—is—John Ermine.'" And the prophet cut the words apart with his forefinger.

John Ermine tried his name again and again, together with other simple expressions. The hermit ceased almost to address him in the Indian tongue. The broad forehead responded promptly to the strain put upon it. Before the snow came, the two had rarely to use the harsh language of the tribesmen. Gradually the pressure was increased, and besides words the hermit imposed ideas. These took root and grew in an alarming way after battling strenuously with those he had imbibed during his youth.

"And why is your name Crooked-Bear, which is Indian, while you are white?"

"My name is not Crooked-Bear except to the Indians; my name is Richard Livingston Merril, though I have not heard the sound of it in many snows and do not care to hear it in many more. You can call me 'Comrade'; that is my name when you speak."

Sitting by their cabin door in the flecked sunlight which the pine trees distributed, the two waded carefully across the lines of some well-thumbed book, taking many perilous flying leaps over the difficult words, but going swiftly along where it was unseasoned Saxon. The prophet longed for a paper and pencil to accelerate the speed, but was forced to content himself with a sharp stick and the smoothed-out dirt before him. At times he sprinkled his sensitive plant with some simple arithmetic; again he lectured on the earth, the moon, and the stars. John Ermine did not leave a flat earth for a round one without a struggle, but the tutor ended up by carving a wooden ball which he balanced in his hand as he separated the sea from the land; he averred that he had known many men who had been entirely around it—which statement could not be disputed.

White Weasel had heard the men speak about the talking-wire and fire-wagon, but he did not believe the tales. John Ermine had more faith, although it puzzled him sorely. Raptly he listened to the long accounts of the many marvels back in the States, and his little Sioux scalp took a new significance as he tried hard to comprehend ten thousand men dying in a single battle of the Great White Man's war. Ten thousand dead men was a severe strain on his credulity when Crooked-Bear imposed it upon him. The ships which fought on the water he did not attempt at all; they were not vivid enough for his contemplation.

When were the white men coming to the Indian lands?

"Before you have a mustache, John Ermine, they will come in numbers as great as the grasshoppers, but you will not care; you are a white man."

Last but not least the prophet removed himself from his Indian pedestal in full sight of his ward. He was no prophet; he was only a man, and a poor specimen at that. Simply, and divested of much perplexity, he taught the Christian religion; told the story of Jesus, and had John Ermine repeat the Ten Commandments, which last the teacher could only marshal after many days of painful reflection, so vagrant are most men's memories as age creeps on.

CHAPTER SEVEN

TRANSFORMATION

FOUR YEARS WERE PASSED BY JOHN ERMINE IN THE CABIN OF THE old man of the mountains, varied by visits to the Absaroke, which grew less frequent as he progressed along the white man's road, rude though the hermit's was. In the reflected light of the prophet he had a more than ordinary influence with the Indians. As his mind expanded, he began to comprehend their simplicity, and exactly why Crooked-Bear, who did not violate their prejudices, could lead them by better paths.

The relationship of the two lonely men grew closer, and under the necessity of the case the hermit took Ermine to a mountain ravine some little distance from his camp. Here he operated a sluice, in connection with a placer, in a desultory way, by which he was able to hive up enough gold dust to fill his wants from the traders. He exacted a promise from the lad that come what would he must never, by word or action, reveal the existence of this place. The hermit wanted only enough to cover his wants during his lifetime, and if no one located the place, Ermine could use it as he saw fit in after years. It would always supply his needs, and when the white men came, as they surely would, the boy might develop the property, but all would be lost without absolute secrecy. Even the Indians did not know of the placer; they always explained to the traders, when questioned concerning the hermit's gold dust, that he made it himself; his medicine was strong, etc. This they believed, and no trader could get farther. Beyond the understanding that gold dust represented the few things necessary to their simple lives, John Ermine cared no more for it than did the blue jays or the Arctic hares. The thing did not interest him beyond a rather intense dislike of the work entailed.

The hermit had often told him the story of himself and his gold. Years ago he had left the States, following the then gentle tide of adventurers who sought fortunes or found death in the unknown hills. He wanted forgetfulness, but his fellows craved gold. On one occasion he formed an alliance with a prospecting miner and an old trapper, relict of the fur-trading days, to go to a place in the Indian country, where the latter had in his wanderings discovered a placer. They outfitted in Lewiston, Idaho, and guided surely by the hunter, had reached the present scene of the hermit's domicile without accident. Finding their hopes realized, they built the log cabin against the rock wall.

As he told it: "We found the quartz-float, and the miner followed it with a gold-pan. We were surprised to find we obtained colors almost from the first. We built the cabin, and put in our spare time in turning the water from the creek to one side of the gulch, so that we could get the sluice-boxes in place, and a proper flow for them, and, at the same time, work the gravel in the bottom of the creek without being inconvenienced by too great a flow of water. All this time we followed the trail to and from the cabin along the rock ledge, where no one but a goat would be apt to find it; and in every way we were careful not to attract wandering Indian hunters to ourselves.

"The miner worked slowly up the creek to where the gold became richer, until it finally petered out. He was then at a loss to account for the disappearance of the metal. This set him to thinking that he must have been working below a ledge where the gold originated. He then began to prospect for the lode itself, which, after due disappointment and effort, we found. It is the ledge which I have shown you, Ermine. The thing was buried in *débris*, and a discoloration of iron stains had confused the miner. He told me that the quartz would go a hundred dollars to the ton, and would make us all rich some day. Of course we did nothing with that, being content, for the present, with the gravel.

"We were high up on the range, away from any divides, and felt safe from wandering Indians. They could discover us only by chance, but by chance they did. One morning, when we had nearly completed the cabin, and were putting on the finishing touches, I was cooking at the fire when I heard a number of gunshots on the outside. I sprang to the half-opened door, and saw my two friends on the ground; one was dead, and the other was rolling about in agony on the pine-needles. A half-dozen Indians rushed out of the timber and soon finished their bloody work. I was so overcome, so unnerved, by the sudden and awful sight, that I could not move my hands or feet. Strangely enough, the Indians did not immediately advance on the cabin, fearing hostile shots. Since then I have found out that they knew by our tracks there were three of us. Taking positions behind trees, they waited. In the still air I could hear them talk to each other. I considered my situation hopeless, but very gradually regained my nerve. Knowing I could not defend the cabin, my mind acted quickly, as often a man's will when he is in such desperate straits. Often I had heard the trapper, who had lived among Indians a great deal during his career, tell of their superstition, their reverence for the unusual, and their tolerance toward such things. At this time I cannot analyze the thought that came to me, but being only half dressed, I tore off my clothes, and getting on all fours, which the unusual length of my arms made possible, I ran out of the cabin, making wild noises and grotesque gestures. My faculties were so shattered at that time that I cannot quite recall all that happened. The Indians did not fire at me, nor did they appear from behind the trees. Growing weary of these antics, and feeling it was best not to prolong the situation, I worked my way toward them. If before this I had been frightened, when I came near two or three of these savages, and could look at them, it was easily seen that they were out of their minds. They were prepared for a man, but not for me. Straightening up, I walked directly to one of them and glared into his eyes. If I looked as wild as I felt, I do not wonder at his amazement. He dropped his gun, and bawled out in his native tongue, which, of course, at that time I did not understand. I answered in a soft voice, which chimed in well with his harsh howling. Presently the others came and gathered round me. I spoke in a declamatory manner for a long time, and one of them addressed some broken English to me.

That man was Half-Moon, whom you know; there is French blood in him, and he had been with the traders, where he had picked up barely enough English to make himself understood.

"He asked me if I was a man, and I said, 'No, I was sent here by the Great Spirit.' I pointed to the sky, and then patted the earth, saying I lived in both places, and that when I had seen them kill white men I had come out of the ground to tell them that the Great Spirit was angry, and that they must not do it again. Oh, when I saw the weather clearing before me, I piled in my trumps; I remembered an actor named Forrest, whom you do not know, of course, but he had a way with him which I copied most accurately.

"The upshot of it all was that I gained their confidence, and felt they would not molest me so long as I could retain it. It was impossible for me to get out of their country, for there was no place in the world that suited me better. All of my worldly possessions were here, and once over the shock of the encounter, I did not especially value my life. You know the rest; no Crow comes near me, or even into this particular locality, except for reasons of Church and State. They have been good to me, and I mean to return it insofar as I can by my superior understanding of the difficulties which beset the tribe. My crooked back served me its only good turn then."

The Sioux and Cheyennes were pressed by the white tide from the south. It came curling in, roller after roller, despite the treaties with their government and in spite of the Indians who rode the country, hunting, shooting, burning, and harassing the invaders. The gold under their feet drew the huge, senseless, irresistible mass of white humanity upon them. It surged over the white soldiers who came to their aid; it flooded around the ends and crept between the crevices. Finally the reprisals of the Indians fused the white soldiers with the gold-hunters: it was war. Long columns of "pony soldiers" and "walk-a-heaps" and still longer lines of canvas-topped wagons trailed snakelike over the buffalo range. The redmen hovered and swooped and burned the dry grass ahead of them, but the fire-spitting ranks crawled hither and yon, pressing the Sioux into the country of the Crows, where great camps were formed to resist the soldiers. The poor Crows fled before them, going into the mountain valleys and inaccessible places to escape the war-ardor of the now thoroughly enraged enemy. These were lean years in the Absaroke lodges. Crooked-Bear and John Ermine dared cook their food only in the midday, fearing their smoke might be more readily seen in the quiet light of morning and evening. They trembled after every shot at game, not knowing to whose ears the sound might carry.

Crows came sneaking into their camp, keen, scared, ghostlike creatures who brought news of the conflict. Bands of Crows had gone with the white men to ride the country in front of them. The white men could not make their own ponies run; they were as dull as buffalo; they travelled in herds, but when they moved forward, no Indians could stop them.

One day, through the shimmering heat, came Wolf-Voice, one of the messengers, with the tale how the Sioux had made a "surround" of pony soldiers on the Ease-ka-poy-tot-chee-archa-cheer and covered a hill with their bodies. But said this one: "Still the soldiers come crawling into the country from all sides. The Sioux and the buffalo run

Wolf-Voice

between them. I am going down the Yellowstone to help the white men. The soldiers make a scout rich."

Crooked-Bear spoke: "John Ermine, now it is time for you to play a man's part; you must go with Wolf-Voice to the soldiers. I would go myself but for my crooked back and the fact that I care nothing for either belligerents; their contentions mean nothing to me. My life is behind me, but yours is in front of you. Begin; go down the valley of the Yellowstone with Wolf-Voice; if the Sioux do not cut you off, you will find the soldiers. Enlist as a scout. I am sure they will take you."

The young man had felt that this hour would arrive, and now that it had come he experienced a particular elation. Early evening found him at the door of the cabin, mounted on one horse and leading his war-pony beside him. The good-by word was all; no demonstration on the part of either man to indicate feelings, although they both were conscious of the seriousness of the parting. The horses disappeared among the trees, and the hermit sat down before his hut, intent at the blank space left by the riders. The revolt of his strong, sensitive nature against his fellows had been so complete that he had almost found happiness in the lonely mountains. While always conscious of an over-whelming loss, he held it at bay by a misanthropic philosophy. This hour brought an acute emptiness to his heart, and the falling shadows of the night brooded with him. Had he completed his work, had he fulfilled his life, was he only to sit here with his pale, dead thoughts, while each day saw the fresh bones of free and splendid animals bleach on the hillsides that he might continue? He was not unusually morbid for a man of his tastes, but his thoughts on this evening were sour. "Bah! The boy may come back; he has the habits of an Indian; he knows how to glide through the country like a coyote. The Sioux will not catch him, and I must wait and hope to see my good work consummated. Nature served that boy almost as scurvy a trick as she did me, but I thwarted her, d—— her!"

CHAPTER EIGHT

PLAYING A MAN'S PART

HE TWO MEN RODE SILENTLY, ONE BEHIND THE other, trailing their led ponies; the hoofs of their horses going out in sound on the pine-needles, anon cracking a dead branch as they stepped over fallen timber, or grunting under the strain of steep hillsides. Far across the wide valley the Shoshone range suddenly lost its forms and melted into blue-black against the little light left by the sun, which sank as a stone does in water. In swift pursuit of her warrior husband, came She of the night, soft and golden, painting everything with her quiet, restful colors, and softly soothing the fevers of day with her cooling lotions.

Wolf-Voice and John Ermine emerged from the woods, dog-trotting along on their ponies after the fashion of Indian kind. Well they knew the deceptions of the pale light; while it illumined the way a few steps ahead, it melted into a protecting gloom within an arrow's-flight. An unfortunate meeting with the enemy would develop a horse-race where numbers counted for no more than the swiftest horse and the rider who quirted most freely over the coulée or dog-town. The winner of such races was generally the one who had the greatest interest at stake in the outcome—the hunted, not the hunter.

As the two riders expected, they traversed the plains without incident, forded the rivers, and two hours before sunrise were safely perched on the opposite range, high enough to look down on the eagles. These vast stretches of landscape rarely showed signs of human life. One unaccustomed to them would as soon expect to find man or horses walking the ocean's bed; their loneliness was akin to the antarctic seas. That was how it seemed, not how it was. The fierce savages who skulked through the cuts and seams made by erosion did not show themselves, but they were there and might appear at any moment; the desert brotherhood knew this, and well considered their footsteps. Seated on a rock pinnacle, amid brushwood, one man slept while the other watched. Long before nightfall they were again in motion. Around the camp, Indians are indolent, but on the warpath their exertions are ceaseless to the point of exhaustion. It was not possible to thread their way through the volcanic gashes of the mountains by night, but while light lasted they skirted along their slopes day after day, killing game with arrows which Wolf-Voice carried because of their silence and economy.

These two figures, crawling, sliding, turning, and twisting through the sunlight on the rugged mountains, were grotesque but harmonious. America will never produce their like again. Her wheels will turn and her chimneys smoke, and the things she makes will be carried round the world in ships, but she never can make two figures which will bear even a remote resemblance to Wolf-Voice and John Ermine. The wheels and chimneys and the white men have crowded them off the earth.

Buckskin and feathers may swirl in the tan-bark rings to the tune of Money Musk, but the meat-eaters who stole through the vast silences, hourly snatching their challenging war-locks from the hands of death, had a sensation about them which was independent of accessories. Their gaunt, hammer-headed, grass-bellied, cat-hammed, roach-backed ponies went with them when they took their departure; the ravens fly high above their intruding successors, and the wolves which sneaked at their friendly heels only lift their suspicious eyes above a rock on a far-off hill to follow the white man's movements. Neither of the two mentioned people realized that the purpose of the present errand was to aid in bringing about the change which meant their passing.

Wolf-Voice had no family tree. It was enough that he arrived among the traders speaking Gros Ventre; but a man on a galloping horse could see that his father was no Gros Ventre; he blew into the Crow camp on some friendly wind, prepared to make his thoughts known in his mother tongue or to embellish it with Breed-French or Chinook; he had sought the camp of the white soldiers and added to his Absaroke sundry "God-damns" and other useful expressions needed in his business. He was a slim fellow with a massive head and a restless soul; a seeker after violence, with wicked little black eyes which glittered through two narrow slits and danced like drops of mercury. His dress was buckskin, cut in the red fashion; his black hat had succumbed to time and moisture, while a huge skinning-knife strapped across his stomach, together with a brass-mounted Henry rifle, indicated the danger zone one would pass before reaching his hair.

At a distance John Ermine was not so different; but, closer, his yellow braids, strongly vermilioned skin, and open blue eyes stared hard and fast at your own, as emotionless as if furnished by a taxidermist. His coat was open at the front as the white men made them; he wore blanket breeches encased at the bottom in hard elkskin leggings bound at the knee. He also carried a fire-bag, the Spencer repeating carbine given him by his comrade, together with an elkhorn whip. In times past Ermine had owned a hat, but long having outlived the natural life of any hat, it had finally refused to abide with him. In lieu of this he had bound his head with a yellow handkerchief, beside which polished brass would have been a dead and lonely brown. His fine boyish figure swayed like a tule in the wind, to the motions of his pony. His mind was reposeful though he was going to war—going to see the white men of whom he had heard so much from his tutor; going to associate with the people who lost "ten thousand men" in a single battle and who did not regard it as wonderful. He had seen a few of these after the Long-Horse fight, but he was younger and did not understand. He understood now, however, and intended to drink his eyes and feast his mind to satiety on the people of whom he was one.

As the sun westered, the two adventurers blinded their trail in the manner most convenient at the time; a thing not so difficult to do in the well-watered northwest as in the dry deserts of the south; besides which the buffalo-hunting, horse-using Indians were not the equals of the mountain foot brethren in following trails. After doing this they doubled and twisted back on their track. While the sun was yet bright they broiled their evening meat on a tiny fire of dry sticks. Blowing the tobacco smoke to the four corners of the earth, Wolf-Voice said: "We will be rich, brother, if the Sioux do not get a chance to dry our hair; the soldiers always make their scouts rich; there is plenty to eat in their wagons, and cartridges cost nothing. The soldiers always fight; they are like the gray bears—they do not know any better—and then is the time when we must watch close to get away before the Sioux have an advantage of them. They are fools and cannot run. They are tied to the ground. If you get a chance to carry the talking papers from one white chief to another, they pour the money into your blanket. I have never had a paper to carry, but I think they will give you one. If they do, brother, we will take the silver and get one of the white soldiers to buy us a bottle of whiskey from the settler." And Wolf-Voice's malignant features relaxed into a peaceful state which made Ermine laugh outright.

A bottle of whiskey and ten thousand dead men—quite a difference, thought Ermine. "That is it—that is it," continued the musing white man to himself; "he goes to war for a bottle of whiskey, and I go for ten thousand men." His unframed thoughts wrestled and twisted, lined and rounded, the idea of ten thousand men; yet the idea never took a form which satisfied him. Ten thousand buffalo—yes, he had calculated their mass; he had seen them. Ten thousand trees—that, too, he could arrange; he had blocked them out on the mountain-side. But there were many times ten thousand men who had not been killed; that he gave up altogether. Nothing had saved him but blind faith in his old comrade.

Leaving the mountains again, they stalked over the moon-lit land more like ghosts than men, and by day they lay so low that the crawling ants were their companions. By the Elk River Wolf-Voice pointed to a long, light streak which passed through the sagebrush: "Brother, that is the sign of the white men. The buffalo, when they pass once, do not make a deeper path than that, and, brother, what is that in the road which shows so bright?"

Appropriating the gleaming thing, the Indian reached from his pony and picked it up, holding it close to his eyes for a moment before passing it to his companion. "What is that, brother?"

Ermine examined it closely, turning it in the moonlight. "I do not know; it is a paper; I will keep it until daylight."

A few steps ahead was found another glistening article, dropped by the passing soldiers. They knew what that was; it was the canteen, lost on the march, by a pony soldier. Wolf-Voice appropriated it.

"We must not stay here; the trail is old, but the Sioux will be near the soldiers. They are between us and the white men; you may be sure of that, brother," said one; and the four ponies stumbled off through the sagebrush, melting into the night.

They stopped for the day at the head of a rocky coulée, eating dried meat for fear of making a smoke. Ermine drew the paper from his pocket, laid it on the ground before him, and regarded it for a few moments; then he turned it round, seeing it was upside down by the writing on the bottom. "Bogardus," he read on the left-hand corner. The image on the card spread, opened, and flowered in Ermine's mind; it was a picture—that was plain now; it was a photograph such as he had heard Crooked-Bear tell about—an image from the sun. He had never seen one before. Wolf-Voice bent his beady eyes on the black and white thing, but it suggested nothing to him. Nature had not been black and white to his scarlet vision. The rude conventional-ized lines painted on the buffalo-robes differentiated buffalo, ponies, and men, but this thing—"Humph!" he lighted his pipe.

Before the persistent gaze of Ermine the face of a young woman unravelled itself from a wonderful headgear and an unknown frock. The eyes looked into his with a long, steady, and hypnotic gaze. The gentle face of the image fascinated the lad; it stirred his imagination and added "a beautiful white woman" to his "ten-thousand-dead-men" quest. Wolf-Voice had to call him twice to take his watch, saying as he lay down, "Put the paper away, brother; it takes your eyes from the Sioux."

The travellers could not make long journeys in the short summer nights through the open country, and exercise a proper vigilance at the same time. The moon rose later every night, thus cutting their time. Neither did they see any signs of human beings or know where to find the white men; but recourse to the trail along the river, from time to time, assured them that the wagons had continued down the stream. The trail was very old, and was full of Indian pony-tracks which had followed it.

One day as they lay in a washout, Wolf-Voice pointed to columns of dust far to the south. Was it buffalo, Indians, or soldiers? The dust stayed all day in one place; it might be a buffalo-surround or big herds about camps, but this they were not able to determine.

"We will go to the dust this sleep and we will ride the war-horses; the others which we have been riding are stiff and sore; we will leave them here and come after them if we can," spoke Ermine as he braided the tail of his favorite pony. When Wolf-Voice's attention was directed elsewhere, he took his medicine, the dried hoof of the white stallion, and rubbed it gently on his pony's heels. The prophet would not approve of this, he felt, but it could do no harm, since he also prayed God to make his pony run fast and not stumble, to blind the Sioux, stop their ears, and otherwise to cherish appropriately the poor life of John Ermine who believed in Him and now wanted His help.

Slowly they made their way south through the gloom, trusting their range-bred ponies to pick out the footing. Hour after hour they stepped along, stopping at intervals to listen.

Late at night as they made their way down a long ridge, they heard a horse whinny somewhere far down in one of the breaks of the land. Without a word they turned away from the noise. Later Wolf-Voice whispered: "Indians; the white men never let their horses loose in the night. That pony was alone, or we should have heard more sounds. He was calling his brothers. Now we must blind our trial; their scouts will find it in the morning."

Accordingly they allowed their horses to feed slowly along, not attempting to guide them, and after a mile felt that any one who should follow those tracks would think that they were loose horses grazing. By the light of the late moon they made their way more quickly, but always stopping to separate the sounds of the night—the good sounds from the bad. They could see that they were coming to the river, and as they rose on a wave of the land, they saw a few faint sparks glitter far down the valley.

"It is the white soldiers—the big fires of the white men, brother. We will go in when the sun comes up. If we should go near them now, they would fire at us. The white men shoot at anything which moves in the dark; a wolf is not safe near their camps when the sun has gone."

Before the gray of morning they were safely ensconced under a bluff, waiting for the daylight and within a mile of the long line of Sibley tents. They heard the hungry mule chorus, the clank of chains, the monotonous calls of the sentries; and the camp slowly developed before their eyes like a photographic negative in a bath of chemicals; then John Ermine began to understand ten thousand men.

Softly the metallic réveille drifted to their ears; it spread from one group of tents to another until the whole air danced with the delightful sound. The watchers on the sagebrush hillside were preoccupied with the movements of the soldiers. They listened to the trumpets and saw the men answer them by forming long lines. In a moment the lines broke into hurrying individuals, the fires began to send up the quiet morning smoke, while the mule chorus ceased.

As though shot out of the ground by some hidden force, Wolf-Voice bounded up. "G——d——! Mit-wit! Coo-ley!" he yelled, and as responsive as a swallow which follows the swift flight of another in play, Ermine bounded on to his horse. One look behind told the story. The Sioux were coming. He saw the lightning play of the ponies' legs, heard the whips crack on their quarters, and was away like a flash, bearing hard on the soldier camp. Before many bounds he recovered from his surprise; it was not far, and his horse was answering the medicine. He had never run like this before. The Sioux had found and followed their trail and had nearly caught them napping. After their long journey they had almost been cut off during the last mile of it. Seeing that their prey had escaped, the Sioux swerved like hawks, pulling up on the hill.

Turning, Wolf-Voice and Ermine shouted back taunts at them, fired their guns at the group, and then leisurely loped toward the

"Halt! Who goes there?"

camps. While yet quite a way out, three white soldiers rose suddenly from a dry wash with their rifles: "Halt! Who goes there?"

The riders drew down to a walk, Wolf-Voice raising his hand in the peace sign, and saying, "We are your frens, we aire two Crow Enjun; don' shoot!" and continued to advance.

The soldiers stood with their guns in readiness, while one answered: "Get off them ponies; lay your guns on the ground. I guess you are all right." And then, looking at Ermine with a laugh: "Is that blonde there a Crow? Guess them Sioux scared him white. I've often heard tell of a man's hair turning white in a single night."

"Ach sure, Bill, and it don't tourn a mon's face red to be schared sthiff," observed another picket.

The faintest suggestion of a smile stole over John Ermine as he comprehended.

"No, soldiers, we are not afraid. Why can't you let two men go into the big camp; are all those soldiers afraid of two men?" And the pickets laughed at the quaint conjecture. Shortly an officer rode up on a horse and questioned Ermine.

"Who are you?"

"We are friends of the white people. Did you see that we are not friends of the Sioux?"

"Yes; I saw those Indians chase you. Were they Sioux?"

"We took that for granted." And again the corner of John Ermine's mouth relaxed.

"Yes, of course, I admire your judgment; come with me," replied the officer, as he turned to ride back. The three ambled along together. "Who are you?"

"I am a white man, and my comrade is an Indian."

"What is your name?"

"My name is John Ermine, and I want to be a scout. Will you take me?"

"That is not my business; but I have no doubt the proper authority will be glad to put you on the pay-roll. You don't seem any more popular with the Sioux than we are."

CHAPTER NINE

IN CAMP

THE THREE HORSEMEN JOGGED INTO CAMP, AND IT CAN HARDLY be stated who was the more impressed by the sight—John Ermine as he passed through the crowds of soldiers, or the soldiers as they looked at the barebacked rider with the yellow braids and the glaring handkerchief. They had left their impedimenta with the worn-out ponies back in the hills with little hope of recovering them. The gathering men who had seen the chase gave tokens of their approval by yelling *Ki-yis* in imitation of the Indians. "Say, Yellow, you're no brevet" "You wa'n't crazy to wait for them Sioux" "The general will feed you on mince-pie" "You'll be a sergeant in the rag-bag troop," and other expressions numerous and 'uncooked' fell on their ears. Ermine felt embarrassed with the attention of so many people centred on him, but his face was cut to stand such shocks. His swift glances about the thronging camp began to illumine the "ten-thousand-men" proposition; he saw lines of tents, wagons without end, but no women; he would have to postpone that feast.

The officer leading stopped in front of a tent around which many officers and men were standing or coming and going. He spoke to one who wore a big hat and a split blond beard, a man less pretentious in his garb than any about him, but whose eye arrested Ermine by the commanding keenness. Dismounting, the officer, saluting, said: "General Crook, these two men were just chased into camp by Indians. They say they are Crows, or at least from the Crows, and they want to be made scouts."

"What Indians chased you?" asked the general.

"We do not know; we were waiting on the hill to come in here by daylight; they surprised us, and we did not stop to talk with them," replied John Ermine.

"Where did you come from, my boy?" he continued.

"I came from the Stinking Water country to help you fight the Sioux—myself and Wolf-Voice there," replied Ermine.

Turning to that waif, the general said, "Who are you?"

Patting his chest impressively, Wolf-Voice spoke: "Me? My mother she was Gro Ventre; I am a warrior; I spak de English; I was scout with Yellow Hair. I am brav mans."

"Umph—no doubt," softly hazarded the Gray Fox. "You were not with him when he died? I suppose you attended to that matter with proper thoroughness. Have you seen any Sioux signs?"

"Yaas—day foliar de wagon, dey aire leave dar pony-track all roun you."

Once fastening his quizzical eyes on the white lad, the general asked, "Do you talk Crow?"

"Yes."

"Can you make the hand talk?"

Ermine gave the sign for "Yes."

"Have you ever been to school?"

"No, sir."

"Who taught you to speak English?"

"My old comrade, Crooked-Bear," said Ermine.

"Crooked-Bear—Crooked-Bear," mused the general. "Oh, I give it up," as he turned away. "You are not one of the Pike County breed, it seems—Crooked-Bear—Crooked-Bear. Take them to the scout camp, Ferguson." And the general retired to his tent, somewhat perplexed by the young man's make-up.

The trio went on toward the scout camp, and as they passed a man on foot he inquired of Ferguson, "Where did you get that pair of aces?"

"The Sioux dealt them to me this morning; will they fill your hand?"

"Yes, sir—think they will." Then to John Ermine, "Do you savvy this country, pardner?"

"Yes, sir; I have always lived in this country," spoke he, with a wave of his arm around the horizon which had the true Indian swing to it, an accomplishment only acquired by white men after long years of association with the tribes. All the signs and gestures made by Indians are distinctive with them and are very suggestive from their constant use of the sign language. The old chief of scouts recognized the significance of the motion on the instant, and knew that one who could make it very probably possessed the other qualifications for his corps.

"What is your name?"

"John Ermine, sir," came the answer. The "sir" had been an acquisition of the last few interviews. He had heard it from the mouth of Crooked-Bear on infrequent occasions, but his quick perceptions told him that it was useful in these canvas towns.

"All right. Will you turn these men over to me for duty, Lieutenant Ferguson?" spoke the chief of scouts, who was a short infantry officer with a huge yellow mustache.

"I will," replied Ferguson, as he turned his horse. "Go with Captain Lewis there; and good luck to you, Mr. Ermine."

After answering certain questions by the chief of scouts, which were intended to prove their fitness for the job, the two late fugitives had the pleasure of knowing that Uncle Sam would open his wagons to them in return for their hair and blood when his representative should order the sacrifice. Wolf-Voice never allowed his mind to dwell on market values, and John Ermine felt that he could do what "ten thousand men" were willing to do in an emergency.

Having done with these formalities, under the trained guidance of Wolf-Voice the two men speedily found their way to the scouts' mess, where they took a hearty toll of the government. About the cook fire squatted or sprawled the allies of the white troops. There were Crows and Indians from other tribes—together with half-breeds whose heraldic emblazonment ought to be a pretty squaw. A few white men came about from time to time, but they did not abide with the regular crew. New faces appeared as they came in from the hills to "cool coffee."

John Ermine walked aimlessly around camp, all eyes and ears. No backwoods boy at a country fair ever had his faculties so over-fed and clogged as he. In turn the soldiers attempted to engage him in conversation as he passed about among them, but the hills had put a seal of silence on his lips; he had not yet found himself amid the bustle.

Captain Lewis

Remarks which grated harshly came to his ears; the unkindness of them undermined the admiration for the white soldiers which the gentle treatment of the officers had instilled.

"Ain't that yellow handkerchief great?" "Sure he'd do well with a hand-organ on the Bowery." "Is he a square shake or a make-up?" and other loose usage of idle minds.

"Say, Bill, come look at the sorrel Injun," sang one trooper to another who stood leaning on a wagon-wheel whittling a stick, to which that one replied: "You take my advice and let the sorrel Injun alone; that butcher knife on his belly is no ornament."

By noon Ermine's mind had been so sloshed and hail-stoned with new ideas that his head was tired. They were coming so fast that he could not stow them, so he found his way back to the scout camp and lay down on a stray robe. The whole thing had not impressed him quite as he had anticipated; it had a raw quality, and he found he did not sift down into the white mass; he had a longing for the quiet of Crooked-Bear's cabin—in short, John Ermine was homesick. However, after a few hours' sleep, he became hungry, which shifted his preoccupation to a less morbid channel.

The scouts talked excitedly of the enemy with whom they had skirmished out on the hills; they discussed the location of the Sioux camp, and speculated on the intention of the Gray Fox. Sunlight or firelight never in the ages played on a wilder group than this; not on the tribes of Asiatics who swarmed in front of Alexander; not in the deserts of Northern Africa: nor on the steppes of Asia, at any period, did sun or fire cut and color cruder men than these who were taking the long, long step between what we know men are and what we think they were.

A soldier stepped briskly into the group, and touching Ermine on the shoulder, said, "The Captain wants to see you; come on." He followed to the tent designated, and was told to come in and sit down. The officer sat opposite, on a camp stool, and after regarding him kindly for a moment, said: "Your name is John Ermine and you are a white man. Where were you born?"

"I do not know, Captain, where I was born, but I have lived all my life with the Crows."

"Yes; but they did not teach you to speak English."

"No; I have lived some years with my old comrade up in the mountains, and he taught me to speak English and to write it."

"Who was your old comrade, as you call him? He must have been an educated man," queried the Captain, looking insistently into Ermine's eyes.

"Captain, I cannot tell, any more than to say that he is an educated white man, who said he is dead, that his fires have burnt out, and he asked me not to speak about him; but you will understand."

Captain Lewis did not understand, nor did he avert his perplexed gaze from Ermine. He was wondering about the boy's mind; had it become deranged? Clearly he saw that Ermine had been a captive; but this mystery of mind cultivation by one who was dead—had he struck a new scheme in psychical research? The Captain rolled a cigarette and scratched a match on the leg of his breeches.

"My old companion told me I ought to come here and help fight the Sioux."

"Have you ever been to war?"

"Yes; I took a scalp from a Sioux warrior when I was a boy, and I wear the eagle feather upright," spoke Ermine in his usual low and measured voice.

"Ho, ho! That is good. I see that you carry a Spencer carbine. I have not seen one lately; we do not use them now."

"It is the best I have, Captain." The Captain took his cigarette from his mouth and bawled: "Jones! *Oh* Jones, Jones!" Almost instantly a soldier stepped into the tent, touching his forehead in salute. "Go down and draw a carbine, fifty rounds, a saddle, blanket, and bridle." Jones disappeared. "Oh, Jones, Jones, and a shirt and hat." Then turning to Ermine, "Do you ever wear shoes?"

"Only this kind I have on, sir."

"Do you want some shoes?"

"No; I think I am better off with these. I have tried on the heavy leather shoes, but they feel as though my feet were caught in a trap."

"Ha, ha! A trap, hey—a good deal so; well, any time you want anything come to me. And now, my boy, may I give you a little advice?"

"You may, sir; I shall be glad of it. I know I have much to learn," assented John Ermine.

"Well, then, you are an odd-looking person even in this camp, and that is saying much, I can assure you. I will have a hat here in a moment which will displace that high-art headgear of yours, and may I ask if you will not take your hair out of those braids? It will be more becoming to you, will not be quite so Injuny, and I think it will not interfere with your usefulness."

"Yes, sir, I will," quietly said the young man, who forthwith undid the plats with a celerity which comes to the owners of long hair. Having finished, he gave his head a toss; the golden tresses, released from their bindings, draped his face, falling down in heavy masses over his shoulders, and the Captain said slowly, "Well, I will be good God-d——d!"

After having soothed his surprise by a repetition of this observation several times, the Captain added, "Say, you are a village beauty, Ermine, by Gad—I'd like a photograph of you." And that worthy continued to feast his eyes on the bewildering sight. It seemed almost as though he had created it.

The orderly entered at this point, loaded down with quartermaster and ordnance stuff. His hat had found its way on to the back of his head during these exertions, and he came up all standing, but the discipline told. All he did as he gazed helplessly at Ermine was to whistle like a bull elk. Quickly recovering himself, "I have the stuff, sir—but—but I'm afraid, sir, the hat won't fit."

"All right, all right, Jones; it will do." And Jones took himself out into the darkness. To a passing comrade he 'unloaded': "Say, Steve, you savvy that blond Injun what was run in here this morning? Well, he's in the Captain's tent, and the Captain has got him to take his hair down, undo them braids, you see; and say, Steve, I am a son-of-a-gun if it ain't like a bushel of hay; say, it's a honey-cooler. You will fall dead when you see it."

Meanwhile Ermine was put in possession of the much-coveted saddle and a new gun, one with a blue barrel without a rust-spot on it anywhere, inside or out. His feelings were only held in leash by a violent repression. The officer enjoyed the proceedings hugely as the young man slipped into the new shirt and tied the yellow handkerchief round his neck. The campaign hat was a failure, as Jones had feared. It floated idly on the fluffy golden tide, and was clearly going to spoil the Captain's art work; it was nothing short of comical. Frantically the officer snatched his own hat from his camp-chest, one of the broad rolling sombreros common on the plains in those days, but now seen no more; this he clapped on Ermine's head, gave it a downward tug together with a pronounced list to the nigh side. Then, standing back from his work, he ran his eyes critically for a moment: "Good! Now you'll do!"

Ermine's serious face found itself able to relax; the ripples broadened over it, his eyes closed, and his mouth opened ever so little, only escaping looking foolish by the fact that he had a reserve; he did not close or broaden too much.

"Well, my boy," said the officer, as he began to put up his papers on the chest, "go down to camp now; the outfit moves tomorrow; you'll do in a free-for-all, by Gad."

When this greeted the easy ears of our hero, he found the loud bustle, so characteristic of the white soldier, more noisy than ever. Slowly the dancing refrain passed from regiment to regiment. The thing itself is dear to the tired soldier who dreads its meaning. It is always a merry beginning, it accords with the freshness of the morning; when associated with youth it never fails to cheer the weary dragging years of him who looks behind.

The tents fluttered down; men ran about their work, munching crackers and hot bacon; they bundled and boxed and heaved things into the escort wagons. Teamsters bawled loudly—it is a concomitant with mule association; yet they were placid about their work of hooking up; their yells never interfered with their preoccupied professionalism. The soft prairie winds sighing through the dreaming teamster's horse-blankets fills his subconscious self with cracks, whistles, howls. "You blaze!" "Oh, Brown!" "D—— you, Brigham!"—,——,——, and other phrases which cannot be printed. That mules and teamsters have never received a proper public appreciation of their importance in war is one of the disheartening injustices of the world. Orderlies and mounted officers tore about; picturesque men who had been saved from the scrap-heap of departing races ranged aimlessly or smoked placidly; they had no packing to do, their baggage was carried in their belts. One of these was John Ermine, who stood by his pony, watching Captain Lewis; this busy man with his multitudinous duties had been picked out for a guiding star. Having presently completed all the details, the Captain mounted and rode away, followed by his motley company. The camp being cleared, the officer turned, and with a wave of his hand which covered the horizon in its sweep, yelled, "Go on now; get to the hell out of here!"

In quick response the wolfish throng broke apart, loping away over the yellow landscape flaming out toward all points; the trained skirmishers trusted their instincts and their horses' heels. John Ermine rode slowly over a hill, and looking backward, saw the long, snakelike columns of horse and foot and wagons come crawling. It was the most impressive sight he had ever beheld, but he could not arrange any plan in his own mind whereby the command was going to fight the Sioux. All the Indians in his world could not and would not try to stem that advance: as well try to stop the falling of the snow or the swarms of grasshoppers. Again, there was no necessity, since the command could no more catch the Sioux than it could reach the sailing hawks or flapping ravens.

Keeping his sharp eyes circling, Ermine mused along. Yes, he remembered what Crooked-Bear had said: "The white men never go back; they do not have to hunt buffalo in order to live; they are paid by the year, and one, two, even a lifetime of years make no difference to them. They would build log towns and scare away the buffalo. The Indians could not make a cartridge or gun," and other things which he had heard came into his mind. It was the awful stolidity of never ending time which appalled Ermine as he calculated his strategy—no single desperate endeavor would avail; to kill all those men behind him would do the Sioux no good whatever. In single battles the white men were accustomed to leave more men than that, dead, on the field. Still, think as he would, the matter was not clear to him. A mile away on his right he saw a friendly scout rise over a bluff; the horse and man made a dot on the dry yellow grass; that was the difference between the solid masses of dust-blown white men behind him and the Indian people; that sight gave him a proportion. If all these white men were dead, it would make no difference; if that Indian on the far-off hill was dead, he could never be replaced.

John Ermine felt one thing above all this abstraction: it was a deep-seated respect for the Sioux personally. Except when a fellow-scout occasionally showed himself on a distant rise, or he looked behind at the dust-pall over the soldiers, there was nothing to be seen of the Sioux; that was another difference, and one which was in no wise reassuring to Ermine. The dry, deserted landscape was, however, an old comrade, and acted as a sedative after the flutter of the camps. The camp held dozy, full-bellied security, but these silences made his ears nervous for a rattle of shots and a pat-a, pat-a, pat-a, of rushing ponies. That is how the desert speaks.

CHAPTER TEN

A Brush with the Sioux

THE DAYS SAW THE BIG SERPENTS OF MEN CRAWL ON AND ON—
hither and yon over the rolling land, saw them splash through
the rivers, wind round the hills, and lie comfortably down at
night. About them fluttered the Indian scouts like flies around a
lamp—hostiles and allies—marking down each other's sign, dashing
in and out, exchanging shots, but always keeping away from the coils
of the serpents.

Many men besides Captain Lewis held out their hands to Ermine,
attracted as they were, first by his picturesque appearance, fine pony,
and seat, and Lewis' enthusiasm; but later by his low-voiced simplicity and acute knowledge concerning the matters about them. They in
turn unravelled many tangled skeins for Ermine; regiments began to
unwind into companies, details, squads; the wagons assorted themselves, and it was not long before the young scout could tell a colonel
from a cook's police at a glance. Numbers of these men had seen the
ten thousand men die, had been with them when they died, had even,
some of them, lain down with them sapped by their own wounds,
though of course they had not died. One big man slapped Ermine on
the back hard enough to make him cough, and said, "I'd rather take
my chance at Cold Harbor than go poking round the hills alone as you
do, my boy." And Ermine had to move away quickly to avoid another
exclamation point, but such little appreciation warmed him. Also the

solidarity of these fellowships took the more definite form of a Colt's revolver, a copy of Upton's tactics, a pocket Bible, a comb from a bald-headed man who respected the unities, together with trifles enough to litter up his saddle-bags.

Old Major Ben Searles in particular used to centre his benevolent eyes on Ermine. He had a boy back in the States, and if he had gone to some other school than West Point might have been a superintendent of an orphan asylum as easily as the soldier which he was. Ermine's quaint questions gave him delicious little mental jolts.

"Why is it, Uncle Ben," asked Ermine, "that all these men come out here to march, get killed, freeze, and starve? They don't have any wives, and I can't see what they have to protect except their eatables."

"You see, Kid, they enlist to do what the government wants them to do, and the government wants them to make the Sioux stop killing white folks just now."

"Yes, but they won't do it. Why don't the government mount them on buffalo ponies, make them eat dried meat, and run after the Sioux instead of taking the villages to war?"

"Well, Ermine, I don't know why. I suppose that is what the Indians would like them to do, and I reckon that is the reason the soldiers don't do it. Soldiers calculate not to do what the enemy wants them to do. Don't you get discouraged; wait a year or two or three, my boy. Oh, we'll get there; we don't know how, but we always stand pat!"

"Pat? Pat? What do you mean by 'standing pat?' Never heard that word. What does it mean?" questioned the young man.

Old Searles laughed. "'Pat' is a word we use in a game of cards, and it means that when you think you are licked you guess you are not. It's a great word, Ermine."

Major Ben Searles

The huge column having crawled over the country as far as it was ordered, broke into divisions, some going down the river in steamboats and other parts through the hills to their far-off posts and cantonments.

The Sioux scouts regarded this as a convenient solution of the awkward situation. Neither they nor the white men could do anything with that unwieldy gathering. Two infantry regiments stayed behind as a reminder to the Sioux that the game was not played out. To one of these Captain Lewis was attached, which good fortune gave Ermine continued employment.

The soldiers began to build winter cantonments at the mouth of the Buffalo Tongue River, or, as the white men called it, "The Tongue," and to gather great quantities of stores which were hauled from Fort Benton. Here was something that the Sioux could attack; they jumped the trains savagely, burned the grass, cut in on the animals to stampede, and peppered up the men as they slept. Stores the troops must have; and though they met repulse at times, they "pounded" the trains through to the Tongue.

It was the custom for wagon trains to go into camp early in the afternoon, which gave the stock a chance to graze while it was yet daylight; it also made it possible to guard them from sudden forays by Indians. On one of these occasions Ermine was with a train which made one of the halts as usual. The Indians had not interfered, and to kill time a few officers, among whom was Searles, started a game of poker. Ermine looked on over their shoulders, trying to comprehend. He had often played the Indian game of "hand," so that poker was merely a new slide between wealth and poverty. Seeing him, Captain Lewis sent him on some trivial errand. While he was gone, an agreement was made to have him come in, and then they were to "Skin him alive" just to see how he would stand it. It worked out beautifully. First they separated what little money he had from his clothes, the officers meanwhile sitting like owls and keeping their faces sober by dint of lip-biting; then the sombrero, which was stacked up as five dollars, found its way to Captain Lewis' head in place of a very bad campaign hat. Next came off the buckskin coat, which was followed by the revolver, and slowly, so that his suspicions might not be aroused, all his personal property, including the saddle and gun, which properly did not belong to him, was laid on the grass beside the victors.

"This is going to be a cold winter, John," laughed one, "or else we'd let you in on that shirt."

"Want to put that pony up for a hundred, Ermine?" asked another.

"No; I'll keep the pony; he's medicine. I've often lost all I had with the plum stones. I guess I don't understand poker." And the young scout arose smiling. The officers laughed themselves into tears, jumped up, and brought comrades to see how they had trimmed John Ermine. Every one greatly enjoyed what they called Ermine's preparations for the winter. He had his government shirt, his blanket breeches, and moccasins left; he had not been so poor since he was a herd-boy, but he had known forms of poverty all his life, so it was not new. What he did not enjoy was his belittlement. The hardworking men in those dangerous, monotonous days were keen for any weakness; and when he heard their laughter he wanted a horse-bucket full of human blood to drown his thoughts. He was greatly disturbed, not so much on account of his losses, although they were everything, as he viewed them, as the ridicule in store for him at Tongue River. There is no greater stimulant to a hardy mind than poverty, and John Ermine's worked like a government-six in a mud-hole, far into the night.

The trio of gamblers, who wore their spoils on their own persons, to the huge edification of the camp, arranged to prolong the torture until they should see the young hatless, coatless, unarmed scout on his barebacked pony during the next march. At the following camp they were to play again, lose to him, and end the joke. Confidences were exchanged, and every one was as tickled as a cur with a new collar.

One of the officers of the poker engagement rode a well-bred American horse of which he was very proud. He had raced it successfully and never declined an opportunity, of which fact Ermine was aware.

It had slowly come to his mind that he had been foully dealt with, so about midnight he jumped up—he had a plan. By dint of daring, fortunate machination, and the coöperation of a quartermaster sergeant whom he took into his confidence, he watered the American horse, fed him with a heavy feed of very salt corn, and later watered him again. The horse had been on short rations and was a glutton. It was with the greatest difficulty that the noble animal managed his breakfast at all; but he was always willing at each opportunity to weaken the saline solution in his stomach.

When the train pulled out, there was Ermine, barebacked and ridiculous. He rode through the volley of jeers and approached the horse-racing officer, saying, "If you are a good gambler, come on; I will run my horse against yours, three arrow-flights and a pitch, horse against horse."

The laughing stopped; here was a new idea—the quarter-bred blood horse, with his sleek bay quarters, against the scout's pony—a good enough animal, but thin and overworked.

The officer halted and stroked his chin with his thumb and forefinger.

"Hum—hum—yes; by Gad, if my horse can't take that runt into camp, he isn't good enough for me. I'll go you."

A cheer went up from those assembled, and some hidden force carried the thrill down the train, which halted. Uncle Sam's business could wait.

The distance was paced off on the level plain; the judges were set; the scouts and officers lined up.

The American's horse's eyes fairly bulged with excitement; he broke into a dripping perspiration, but seemingly no one noticed this but Ermine. He knew that the load of water would choke him in twenty yards.

The old war-pony was thin from overwork, but responsive as a dog to his bareback rider, and dangerous-looking to one used to see ponies which show worse in condition than out, by reason of the ungraceful architectural lines.

The pistol spoke; the pony gained three jumps from the mark. The American made the best of a bad job, but Ermine was able to turn at the finish and back him over the judges' line.

The officer nearly had apoplexy, as he pulled up. He threw himself off the horse and handed the reins to Ermine.

The action of both challenge and race had been so rapid and so badly calculated on the officer's part that he lacked time to assimilate the idea that he was a fool. He tried to maintain a composure which was lacking, as every one could see.

"If you will get all my clothes, saddle, and gun back from your comrades, I will give you your horse," said the scout.

The spectators who knew about the poker game now sat howling hopelessly on their horses' backs. Searles and the others now came to their beaten friend's aid; they shed their plunder in front of Ermine's horse, produced the saddle and gun from a nearby escort wagon, laid them carefully down with the rest, and the victor granted peace.

"Here is your horse," said Ermine, and he laughed.

The occurrence had a serious side; the three officers were quick to appreciate that. Searles stood in front of the scout and made utterance: "I want to say before all these men that the poker game was not on the square—that we robbed you purposely for a joke, and that we intended to give your property back to you tonight; and I call on all these men to witness my remarks."

"Yes, yes," came the chorus; "it was all a joke. Searles said he would give it back. Don't hold it out against him, Ermine," and other reassuring remarks. They recognized the young scout's magnanimity as a conqueror.

The laughing ceased; the thing evidently had been carried too far. It would not sound well when told at Tongue River. The unfortunate horse-race had made proper restitution impossible.

By this time John Ermine had his clothing and saddle arranged and was mounted. He spoke:

"Well, if that is so, if it only was a joke, I suppose I ought to say that I sat up half of last night salting your horse. Look at him! He is blowing yet; he is as full of water as a drowned buffalo. I am glad it did not kill him; let us bury the axe."

Major Searles and his fellows were unlike many jokers; they slowly readjusted after the shock and laughed with the others.

The march was resumed, but the customary monotony of this slow pacing of interminable landscape was often abruptly broken by individuals ha-haing loudly, as the sequence of events took a new hold of their risibles; and Mr. John Ermine tightened in an ever increasing hold on their fancies.

Major Searles, riding beside his horse-racing *confrère*, tried to cheer him. "Brace up, compadre; that boy has you buffaloed. We are all right; we are nothing but a bunch of monkeys. The only thing we forgot was that a fellow who has lived all his life with Injuns is likely to know how to gamble and race horses. He'll be wanting to juggle the bone for us yet, and we are bound to go him."

"You bet," came the reply; "he has got us staked out, and he can come along and do jig steps on our chest any time he feels like it. That is where we have to moisten our lips and look pleasant, too."

An old wagon boss sauntered by on his mule with its mouth *à la crocodile.*

"Ha, ha! Reckon you fellers has had all the fun that's a-comin' to you. That boy had that last deck marked, bottomed, sanded, and pricked, with more up his sleeve and some in the back of his neck."

John Ermine and Wolf-Voice, meanwhile, had gone well out in front of the train, loping this way and that about the course of advance, with eyes for everything.

Presently they were seen to stop, turn, and come back, flying as fast and straight as the antelope runs.

"How now, by Gad! Here's smoke for us!" said Searles. No one laughed any more.

Swift and noiseless as the birds came the scouts; nearer and nearer, until their flying horses' hair could be seen; then sounded the hoof-beats until they drew rein. Wolf-Voice's hair fairly stood up, and his fierce little eyes danced attendance; he talked all the languages he knew, and worked his free hand in most alarming sign signals to help his expression.

"What's up, Ermine?" said the Major.

"Well, Major, the ground out there is alive with fresh pony-tracks. I think you had better bunch up."

The train was strung out, having passed a bad "draw." Turning, the Major shouted: "Close up in columns of fours! Deploy that escort out!"

The order flew down the train; the whips cracked, and the straining mules trotted into position; the infantry guard ran out from the sides, shoving shells into the breech-blocks. Even while this was in motion, a torrent of Sioux poured over the bluffs, back of the flat, and came on.

The soldiers dropped on to their knees in the sagebrush. The Major spurred to the particular point for which they were headed, followed by scouts and several mounted men.

"Steady, men! Hold your fire!"

The men were aiming, and each had five cartridges in his teeth. In a sonorous roll came, "Steady—steady—steady!" And the gay stream of savagery bore on.

"Fire!" Like a double drag on a drum which gradually dies, the rifles rattled down the extended line, all concentrated on the head of the flying column. The smoke played along the gray sage; there was a sharp clatter of breech-blocks, and an interval.

"Ready! Fire!" and this repeated.

The Major jogged to a windblown place and saw that the column had veered to its right but was not checked. Followed by his few mounted men, he rode along behind their line parallel with the head of the charge, but before the slow and steady fire the Indian line drew out. The train was caught in the circle, but the enemy had not the heart to ride over the deadly skirmish line. The close columns of wagons now turned off down toward the river, and, keeping their distances, the infantry followed it. Indian ponies lay kicking out on the dry plain, and here and there could be seen warriors who retired slowly from the racing Indians; they had been plugged.

Bullets kicked up the dust, and one or two soldiers had to be helped along by their comrades.

The heated air shimmered over the land; but for the rattle and thud of gun and pony, the clank, snort, and whip-cracks among the wagons, the great, gray plains lay silent.

No eye save that of a self-considering golden eagle looked on, and he sailed placidly far above. Ponies and mules strained and lathered, men sweated and grunted and banged to kill; nature lay naked and insensate.

The Indians made a stand under the cut banks of the river, but were flanked out. The train drove slowly into a corral form, when the mules were unhooked. The guard began to rifle-pit among the wagons, and the Indians drew off to breathe their ponies. They had stopped the train, but the "walk-a-heap" soldiers were behind the wagons, which

"*Bullets kicked up the dust*"

were full of "chuck," and water was at hand. Indians always dreaded the foot-soldiers, who could not run away, and who would not surrender, but worked their long rifles to the dying gasp; they were "heap bad medicine"; they were like wounded gray bears in a den of rocks—there was no reasonable method for their capture.

Major Searles jumped from his horse, took off his hat, and mopped his forehead with his handkerchief. "So far, so good! So far, so good! But not so very d—— far either," he mused.

Towing his pony behind him, Wolf-Voice came up, legs bowed and wobbly, horseback fashion when afoot. Calling loudly, he said:

"By Jeskris, Maje Searl, bout two-tree minit you bettar look out; dose Kul-tus-til-akum she mak de grass burn yu up, by Gar. Win' she waas come deese way."

"Yes—yes, that's right. Here you, Ermine, and you, Lieutenant Smith, take what men you want and kill a wounded mule—drag his hide over the grass to windward; it is short and won't burn high. And, Lieutenant, give me all the men you can over here; they will try to come through the smoke." Saying which, the Major made his way to the ammunition wagons and had the mules hooked to them, intending to run these into the river in case the fire came through.

In fighting Indians, the Major, who was an old hand, knew that one must act quickly, for they are rapid tacticians and their blows come fast.

These preparations had no sooner been made than, true to Wolf-Voice's admonitions, the Indians came down, and, just out of rifle-range, started the fire down wind. Almost no air was stirring; the flames ran slowly through the short buffalo-grass, but weeds and sage made considerable smoke, which came toward the train.

The dripping carcass of the mule was dragged in a ring round the windward side of the train; the smoke eddied over the wagons; the Indians could not be seen; every man's eyes and ears were strained and fingers twitched as they lay at an "aim" or "ready," among the wagon-wheels.

The mules grew restive and sat back on their fastenings; but there, matters had been well attended to, for the side-lines and hobbles were leathered and laced.

To the silent soldiers this was one of the times when a man lives four years in twenty minutes; nothing can be compared to it but the prolonged agony between your "Will you have me?" and her "yes" or "NO."

As the fire came nearer, they heard its gentle crackle, crackle; their nerves all crackled in unison. It reached the bloody ring left by the poor mule—"would the d—— Injuns never come?" At the guard line the flames died and crackled no more. The smoke grew thinner, and at last they saw out through it; the Indians held themselves safely out of rifle-shot.

"Hum," said Searles, as he stepped down from a wagon-wheel, "they didn't want any of this chicken pie." And then he did what he was never known to do under ordinary circumstances; and when he was through, the men cheered, and every mule-skinner who had heard him envied a man who could talk it off just like that.

"Ah, Maje Searl," chimed in Wolf-Voice, "don' you been scare; dose Injuns no say goo'by yet, mabeso."

And they did not say good-by. They dismounted and went behind the washes in the shallow river. They peppered and banged the men as they watered the stock, the perilous trip only being made behind a strong skirmish line with three men hit and a half-dozen mules. The soldiers ate a quiet supper and put out the fires before the sun went down. The Indians, with the declining light, crawled in on the train and pecked at the monster.

"Pe-e-e-eing" went a bullet on a wagon-tire; "slap" went another on a wagon box; "thud," as one buried in a grain-bag; "phud," and the ball made a mule grunt; but the echoing Springfields spit their 45's at the flashes.

Searles sent for Ermine and Wolf-Voice, and sitting on the grass behind a barricade of grain-sacks, he began: "We are corralled, and I haven't escort enough to move. I can hold out till snow, but can't graze my stock. Some one has to go back for reënforcements. Will you go? It can be made on a good horse by moving."

"Well, Major, I'll try it. I can go if I can get through with a fair start. The moon will come up later, and I must go now while there is a chance," said Ermine.

"Will you go also, Mr. Wolf-Voice?"

"Well, hit be good chance for geet keel. Yaes, I go, mebeso, feefty doaller," vouchsafed that worthy, after nicely balancing the chances.

"What do you want for going, John Ermine?" asked the Major.

"I don't want anything. I came to fight the Sioux. I do not go to war for fifty dollars." But it was too dark for the half-breed to see the contempt in Ermine's face, so he only shrugged his shoulders and contented himself with, "Oh, weel, mabeso dose soldier-man go for not so much. I do not."

"All right, all right! I'll give you an order for fifty dollars. Here are the papers." And the Major handed one to each. "Now, don't lose them, whatever else you do."

"Ma pony, she steef, no good. I was go on de foot." And Wolf-Voice proceeded to skin off his motley garments. In these desperate situations he believed in the exemplar of his name; its methods were less heroic but more sure.

Ermine half stripped himself, and his horse wholly; bound up the tail, and in the gloom rubbed the old dried horse's hoof on his heels. It had, at least, never done any harm, and at times favored him. Sak-a-war-te and the God of the white men—he did not know whether they were one or two. Trusting his valuables to the care of the Major, he was let out of the corral after a good rattle of firing, into the darkness, away from the river.

Only a few rifles ripped the night air in response to this, which he took to indicate that the better part of the Indians were along the river. He glided away, leading his pony, and the last the soldiers saw was the flash of a gun turned in an opposite direction from the wagon train. Neither Wolf-Voice or Ermine again appeared.

The slow fight continued during the night and all the next day, but by evening the Indians disappeared. They had observed the approach of reënforcements, which came in during the following morning, led by Ermine. Wolf-Voice, who had been on foot, did not make the rapid time of his mounted partner, but had gone through and acquired the fifty dollars, which was the main object.

CHAPTER ELEVEN

THE TRUTH OF THE EYES

THE SOLDIERS WHO HAD BEEN IN THE WAGON-TRAIN fight carried John Ermine's fame into cantonments, and Major Searles never grew tired of the pæan:

> I do not go to war for fifty dollars,
> You can bet your boots that isn't not me lay.
> When I fight, it's only glory which I collars,
> Also to get me little beans and hay.

But his more ardent admirers frowned on this doggerel, and reminded the songsters that no one of them would have made that courier's ride for a thousand acres of Monongahela rye in bottles. As for Wolf-Voice, they appreciated his attitude. "Business is business, and it takes money to buy marbles," said one to another.

But on the completion of the rude huts at the mouth of the Tongue, and when the last wagon train had come through, there was an ominous preparation for more serious things. It was in the air. Every white soldier went loping about, doing everything from greasing a wagon to making his will.

"Ah, sacre, John," quoth Wolf-Voice, "am much disturb; dese Masta-Shella waas say dis big chief—what you call de Miles? She medicin fighter; she very bad mans; she keep de soldiers' toes sore all de taime. She no give de dam de cole-moon, de yellow-grass moon; she hump de Sioux. Why for we mak to trouble our head? We have dose box, dose bag, dose barrel to heat, en de commissaire—wael 'nough grub las' our lifetaime; but de soldier say sure be a fight soon; dat Miles she begin for paw de groun'—it be sure sign. Wael, we mak' a skin dat las fight, hey, John?"

Ermine in his turn conceived a new respect for the white soldiers. If their heels were heavy, so were their arms when it came to the final hug. While it was not apparent to him just how they were going to whip the Sioux and Cheyenne, it was very evident that the Indians could not whip the soldiers; and this was demonstrated directly when Colonel Miles, with his hardy infantry, charged over Sitting Bull's camp, and while outnumbered three to his one, scattered and drove the proud tribesmen and looted their tepees. Not satisfied with this, the grim soldier crawled over the snow all winter with his buffalo-coated men, defying the blizzards, kicking the sleeping warriors out of their blankets, killing and chasing them into the cold starvation of the hills. So persistent and relentless were the soldiers that they fought through the captured camps when the cold was so great that the men had to stop in the midst of battle to light fires, to warm their fingers, which were no longer able to work the breech-locks. Young soldiers cried in the ranks as they perished in the frigid atmosphere; but notwithstanding, they never stopped. The enemy could find no deep defile in the lonely mountains where they were safe; and entrench where they would among the rocks, the steady line charged over them, pouring bullets and shell. Ermine followed their fortunes and came to understand the dying of "the ten thousand men." These people went into battle with the intention of dying if not victorious. They never consulted their heels, no matter what the extremity. By the time of the green grass the warriors of the northern plains had either sought their agencies or fled to Canada. Through it all Ermine had marched and shot and frozen with the rest. He formed attachments for his comrades—that enthusiastic affection which men bring from the camp and battlefield, signed by suffering and sealed with blood.

CHAPTER TWELVE

KATHERINE

T HE SNOW HAD GONE. THE PLAINS AND BOXLIKE BLUFF AROUND the cantonments had turned to a rich velvet of green. The troops rested after the tremendous campaigns in the snow-laden, windswept hills, with the consciousness of work well done. The Indians who had been brought in during the winter were taking their first heart-breaking steps along the white man's road. The army teams broke the prairie, and they were planting the seed. The disappearance of the buffalo and the terrible white chief Bear-Coat, who followed and fought them in the fiercest weather, had broken their spirits. The prophecies of the old beaver-men, which had always lain heavily on the Indian mind, had come true at last—the whites had come; they had tried to stop them and had failed.

The soldiers' nerves tingled as they gathered round the landing. They cheered and laughed and joked, slapped and patted hysterically, and forgot the bilious officialism entirely.

Far down the river could be seen the black funnel of smoke from the steamboat—their only connection with the world of the white men. It bore letters from home, luxuries for the mess-chest, and best of all, news of the wives and children who had been left behind when they went to war.

Every one was in a tremor of expectancy except the Indians, who stood solemnly apart in their buffalo-robes, and John Ermine. The steamboat did not come from their part of the world, and brought nothing to them; still Ermine reflected the joyousness of those around him, and both he and the Indians knew a feast for their eyes awaited them.

In due course the floating house—for she looked more like one than a boat—pushed her way to the landing, safe from her thousand miles of snags and sandbars. A cannon thudded and boomed. The soldiers cheered, and the people on the boat waved handkerchiefs when they did not use them to wipe happy tears away; officers who saw their beloved ones walked to and fro in caged impatience. When the gang-planks were run out, they swarmed aboard like Malay pirates. Such hugging and kissing as followed would have been scandalous on an ordinary occasion; lily white faces were quite buried in sunburnt mustaches on mahogany-brown skins. The unmarried men all registered a vow to let no possible occasion to get married escape them, and little boys and girls were held aloft in brawny arms paternal. A riot of good spirits reigned.

"For Heaven's sake, Mary, did you bring me my summer underwear?"

"Oh, don't say you forgot a box of cigars, Mattie."

"If you have any papers or novels, they will save me from becoming an idiot," and a shower of childish requests from their big boys greeted the women.

In truth, it must be stated that at this period the fashion insisted upon a disfigurement of ladies which must leave a whole generation of noble dames forgotten by artists of all time. They loosened and tightened their forms at most inappropriate places; yet underneath this fierce distortion of that bane of woman, Dame Fashion, the men were yet able to remember there dwelt bodies as beautiful as any Greek ever saw or any attenuated Empire dandy fancied.

"Three cheers for the first white women on the northern buffalo range!"

"See that tent over there?" asked an officer of his 'Missis,' as he pointed toward camp; "well, that's our happy home; how does it strike you?"

A bunch of "shave-tails" were marched ashore amid a storm of good-natured raillery from the "vets" and mighty glad to feel once again the grit under their brogans. Roustabouts hustled bags and boxes into the six-mule wagons. The engine blew off its exhaust in a frail attempt to drown the awful profanity of the second mate, while humanity boiled and bubbled round the great river-box.

The Indians stood motionless, but their keen eyes missed no details of the strange medley. Ermine leaned on a wagon-tail, carefully paring a thin stick with a jack-knife. He was arrayed for a gala day in new soldier trousers, a yellow buckskin shirt beautifully beaded by the Indian method, a spotted white handkerchief around his neck, buckskin leggings on the lower leg above gay moccasins, a huge skinning-knife and revolver in his belt, and a silver watch chain. His golden hair was freshly combed, and his big rakish sombrero had an eagle feather fastened to the crown, dropping idly to one side, where the soft wind eddied it about.

The John Ermine of the mountain den was a June-bug beside this butterfly, but no assortment of color can compete with a scarlet blanket when the clear western sun strikes on it; so in consequence Ermine was subdued by Wolf-Voice, who stood beside him thus arrayed.

As the people gathered their bags and parcels, they came ashore in small groups, the women and children giving the wild Indians the heed which their picturesque appearance called for, much of this being in the form of little shivers up and down the spine. A true old wolf-headed buffalo Indian would make a Japanese dragon look like a plate of ice cream, and the Old Boy himself would have to wave his tail, prick up his sharp ears, and display the best of his Satanic learning to stand the comparison.

Major Searles passed on with the rest, beaming like a June morning, his arms full of woman's equipment—Mrs. Searles on one side and his daughter on the other.

"Hello, Ermine."

"How do, Major?" spoke the scout as he cast his whittling from him.

"This is John Ermine, who saved my life last winter, my dear. This is Mrs. Searles, John."

She bowed, but the scout shook hands with her. Miss Searles, upon presentation, gave Ermine a most chilling bow, if raising the chin and dropping the upper eyelids can be so described; and the man who pushed his pony fearlessly among the whirling savages recoiled before her batteries and stood irresolute.

Wolf-Voice, who had not been indicated by the Major, now approached, his weird features lighted up with what was intended as pleasantry, but which instead was rather alarming.

"How! How me heap glad to see you." And to Miss Searles, "How! How you heap look good." After which they passed on.

"My, my, papa, did you ever see such beautiful hair as that man Ermine has?" said Katherine Searles. "It was a perfect dream."

"Yes, good crop that—'nough to stuff a mattress with; looks better today than when it's full of alkali dust," replied the Major.

"If the young man lost his hat, it would not be a calamity," observed the wife.

Katherine

"And, papa, who was that dreadful Indian in the red blanket?"

"Oh, an old scoundrel named Wolf-Voice, but useful in his place. You must never feed him, Sarah, or he will descend on us like the plague of locusts. If he ever gets his teeth into one of our biscuits, I'll have to call out the squad to separate him from our mess-chest."

A strange thought flashed through John Ermine's head—something more like the stroke of an axe than a thought, and it had deprived him of the power of speech. Standing motionless and inert, he watched the girl until she was out of sight. Then he walked away from the turmoil, up along the riverbank.

Having gained a sufficient distance, he undid the front of his shirt and took out a buckskin bag, which hung depended from his neck. It contained his dried horse's hoof and the photograph of a girl, the one he had picked up in the moonlight on the trail used by the soldiers from Fort Ellis.

He gazed at it for a time, and said softly, "They are the same, that girl and this shadow." And he stood scrutinizing it, the eyes looking straight into his as they had done so often before, until he was intimate with the image by a thousand vain imaginings. He put it back in his bag, buttoned his shirt, and stood in a brown study, with his hands behind his back, idly stirring the dust with the point of one moccasin.

"It must have been—it must have been Sak-a-war-te who guided me in the moonlight to that little shadow paper there in the road—to that little spot in all this big country; in the nighttime and just where we cut that long road; it means something—it must be." And he could get no farther with his thoughts as he walked to his quarters.

Along the front of the officers' row he saw the bustle, and handshaking, laughter, and quick conversation. Captain Lewis came by with a tall young man in citizen's clothes, about whom there was a blacked, brushed, shaved appearance quite new on the Tongue.

"I say, and who is that stunning chap?" said this one to Lewis, in Ermine's hearing.

"One of my men. Oh, come here, Ermine. This is Mr. Sterling Harding, an Englishman come out to see this country and hunt. You may be able to tell him some things he wants to know."

The Englishman

The two young men shook hands and stood irresolutely regarding each other. Which had the stranger thoughts concerning the other or the more curiosity cannot be stated, but they both felt the desire for better acquaintance. Two strangers on meeting always feel this—or indifference, and sometimes repulsion. The relations are established in a glance.

"Oh, I suppose, Mr. Ermine, you have shot in this country."

"Yes, sir," Ermine had extended the "sir" beyond shoulder-straps to include clean shirts—"I have shot most every kind of thing we have in this country except a woman."

"Oh! Ha! Ha ha!" And Harding produced a cigar-case.

"A woman? I suppose there hasn't been any to shoot until this boat came. Do you intend to try your hand on one? Will you have a cigar?"

"No, sir; I only meant to say I had shot things. I suppose you mean have I hunted."

"Yes, yes—exactly; hunted is what I mean."

"Well then, Mr. Sterling Harding, I have never done anything else."

"Mr. Harding, I will leave you with Ermine; I have some details to look after. You will come to our mess for luncheon at noon?" interjected Captain Lewis.

"Yes, with pleasure, Captain." Whereat the chief of scouts took himself off.

"I suppose, Mr. Ermine, that the war is quite over, and that one may feel free to go about here without being potted by the aborigines," said Harding.

"The what? Never heard of them. I can go where I like without being killed, but I have to keep my eyes skinned."

"Would you be willing to take me out? I should expect to incur the incidental risks of the enterprise," asked the Englishman, who had taken the incidental risks of tigers in India and sought "big heads" in many countries irrespective of dangers.

"Why, yes; I guess Wolf-Voice and I could take you hunting easily enough if the Captain will let us go. We never know here what Bear-Coat is going to do next; it may be 'boots and saddles' any minute," replied the scout.

"Oh, I imagine, since Madam has appeared, he may remain quiet and I really understand the Indians have quite fled the country," responded Harding.

"Mabeso; you don't know about Indians, Mr. Harding. Indians are uncertain; they may come back again when their ponies fill up on the green grass."

"Where would you propose to go, may I ask?"

Ermine thought for a time, and asked, "Would you mind staying out all one moon, Mr. Harding?"

"One moon? You mean thirty days. Yes, three moons, if necessary. My time is not precious. Where would you go?"

"Back in the mountains—back on the Stinking Water; a long way from here, but a good place for the animals. It is where I come from, and I haven't been home in nearly a year. I should like to see my people," continued Ermine.

"Anywhere will do; we will go to the Stinking Water, which I hope belies its name. You have relatives living there, I take it."

"Not relatives; I have no relations anywhere on the earth, but I have friends," he replied.

"When shall we start?"

Ermine waved his hand a few times at the sky and said "So many," but it failed to record on the Englishman's mind. He was using the sign language. The scout noted this, and added, "Ten suns from now I will go if I can."

"Very well; we will purchase ponies and other necessaries mean-while, and will you aid me in the preparations, Mr. Ermine? How many ponies shall we require?"

"Two apiece—one to ride and the other to pack," came the answer to the question.

A great light dawned upon Harding's mind. To live a month with what one Indian pony could carry for bedding, clothes, cartridges, and food. His new friend failed, in his mind, to understand the require-ments of an English gentleman on such quests.

"But, Mr. Ermine, how should I transport my heads back to this point with only one pack-animal?"

"Heads? Heads? Back here?" stumbled the light-horseman. "What heads?"

"Why, the heads of such game as I might be so fortunate as to kill."

"What do you want of their heads? We never take the heads. We give them to our little friends, the coyotes," queried Ermine.

"Yes, yes, but I must have the heads to take back to England with me. I am afraid, Mr. Ermine, we shall have to be more liberal with our pack-train. However, we will go into the matter at greater length later."

Sterling Harding wanted to refer to the Captain for further understanding of his new guide. He felt that Lewis could make the matter plain to Ermine by more direct methods than he knew how to employ. As the result of worldwide wanderings, he knew that the Captain would have to explain to Ermine that he was a crazy Englishman who was all right, but who must be humored. To Harding this idea was not new; he had played his blood-letting ardor against all the forms of outlandish ignorance. The savages of many lands had eaten the bodies of which the erratic Englishman wanted only the heads.

So to Lewis went Harding. "I say, Captain, your Ermine there is an artless fellow. He is proposing to Indianize me, to take me out for a whole moon, as he calls it, with only one pack-pony to carry my belongings. Also he fails, I think, to comprehend that I want to bring back the heads of my game."

"Ha! I will make that plain to him. You see, Mr. Harding, you are the first Englishman he ever encountered; fact is he is range bred, unbranded and wild. I have ridden him, but I use considerable discretion when I do it, or he would go up in the air on me," explained Lewis. "He is simple, but he is honest, faithful, and one of the very few white men who know this Indian country. Long ago there were a great many hunters and trappers in these parts; men who worked for the fur companies, but they have all been driven out of the country of late years by the Indians, and you will be lucky to get Ermine. There are plenty of the half-breeds left, but you cannot trust them. They might steal from you, they might abandon you, or they might kill you. Ermine will probably take you into the Crow country, for he is solid with those people. Why, half the time when I order Crow scouts to do something they must first go and make a talk with Ermine. He has some sort of a pull with them—God knows what. You may find it convenient to agree with him at times when you naturally would not; these fellows are independent and follow their fancies pretty much. They don't talk, and when they get an idea that they want to do anything, they proceed immediately to do it. Ermine has been with me nearly a year now, but I never know what minute I am to hear he has pulled out."

Seeing Ermine some little distance away, the Captain sent an orderly after him. He came and leant with one hand on the tent pole of the fly.

"Ermine, I think you had better take one or two white packers and at least eight or ten animals with you when you go with Mr. Harding."

"All right, sir, we can take as many packers as he likes, but no wagons."

Having relieved the scout of his apprehensions concerning wagons, the bond was sealed with a cigar, and he departed, thinking of old Crooked-Bear's prediction that the white men would take him to their hearts. Underneath the happy stir of his faculties on this stimulating day there played a new emotion, indefinite, undefinable, a drifting, fluttering butterfly of a thought which never alighted anywhere. All day long it flitted, hovered, and made errant flights across his golden fancies—a glittering, variegated little puff of color.

CHAPTER THIRTEEN

PLAYING WITH FIRE

O N THE FOLLOWING MORNING HARDING HUNTED UP JOHN
Ermine, and the two walked about together, the Englishman
trying to fire the scout with his own passion for strange lands
and new heads.

To the wild plainsman the land was not new; hunting had its old
everyday look, and the stuffed heads of game had no significance. His
attention was constantly interrupted by the little flutter of color made
more distinct by a vesper before the photograph.

"Let us go and find your friend, Wolf-Voice," said Harding, which
they did, and the newcomer was introduced. The Englishman threw
kindly, wondering eyes over the fiercely suspicious face of the half-
breed, whose evil orbs spitted back at him.

"Ah, yees—you was go hunt. All-right; I weel mak' you run de buffalo, shoot dose elk, trap de castor, an you shall shake de han' wid de
grizzly bear. How much money I geet—hey?"

"Ah, you will get the customary wages, my friend, and if you give
me an opportunity to shake hands with a grizzly, your reward will be
forthcoming," replied the sportsman.

"Very weel; keep yur heye skin on me, when you see me run lak
hell—weel, place where I was run way from, dare ees mousier's grizzly
bear, den you was go up shake han', hey?"

Harding laughed and offered the man a cigar, which he handled
with four fingers much as he might a tomahawk, having none of the
delicate art native to the man of cigars or cigarettes. A match was

proffered, and Wolf-Voice tried diligently to light the wrong end. The Englishman violently pulled Ermine away, while he nearly strangled with suppressed laughter. It was distinctly clear that Wolf-Voice must go with them.

"Your friend Wolf-Voice seems to be quite an individual person."

"Yes, the soldiers are always joshing him, but he doesn't mind. Sometimes they go too far. I have seen him draw that skinning-knife, and away they go like a flock of birds. Except when he gets loaded with soldier whiskey, he is all right. He is a good man away from camp," said Ermine.

"He does not appear to be a thoroughbred Indian," observed Harding.

"No, he's mixed; he's like that soup the company cooks make. He is not the best man in the world, but he is a better man in more places than I ever saw," said Ermine, in vindication.

"Shall we go down to the Indian camp and try to buy some ponies, Ermine?"

"No, I don't go near the Sioux; I am a kind of Crow. I have fought with them. They forgive the soldiers, but their hearts are bad when they look at me. I'll get Ramon to go with you when you buy the horses. Ramon was a small trader before the war, used to going about with a half-dozen packhorses, but the Sioux ran him off the range. He has pack saddles and rawhide bags, which you can hire if you want to," was explained.

"All right; take me to Ramon if you will."

"I smoke," said Ermine as he led the way.

Having seen that worthy depart on his trading mission with Harding in tow, Ermine felt relieved. Impulse drew him to the officers' row, where he strolled about with his hands in his cartridge-belt. Many passing by nodded to him or spoke pleasantly. Some of the newly arrived ladies even attempted conversation; but if the soldiers of a year ago were difficult for Ermine, the ladies were impossible. He liked them; their gentle faces, their graceful carriage, their evident interest in him, and their frank address called out all his appreciation. They were a revelation after the squaws, who had never suggested any of these possibilities. But they refused to come mentally near him, and he did not know the trail which led to them. He answered their questions, agreed with whatever they said, and battled with his diffidence until he made out to borrow a small boy from one mother, proposing to take him down to the scout camp and quartermaster's corral to view the Indians and mules.

He had thought out the proposition that the Indians were just as strange to the white people as the white people were to them, consequently he saw a social opening. He would mix these people up so that they could stare at each other in mutual perplexity and bore one another with irrelevant remarks and questions.

"Did Mr. Butcher-Knife miss Madam Butcher-Knife?" asked a somewhat elderly lady on one occasion, whereat the Indian squeezed out an abdominal grunt and sedately observed to "Hairy-Arm," in her own language, that "the fat lady could sit down comfortably," or words that would carry this thought.

The scout who was acting as their leader upon this occasion emitted one loud "A-ha!" before he could check himself. The lady asked what had been said. Ermine did not violate a rule clearly laid down by Crooked-Bear, to the effect that lying was the sure sign of a man's worthlessness. He answered that they were merely speaking of something which he had not seen, thus satisfying his *protégé*.

After a round or two of these visits this novelty was noised about the quarters, and Ermine found himself suddenly accosted. By his side was the original of his cherished photograph, accompanied by Lieutenant Butler of the cavalry, a tall young man whose body and movements had been made to conform to the West Point standards.

"Miss Searles has been presented, I believe. She is desirous of visiting the scout camp. Would you kindly take us down?"

John Ermine's soul drifted out through the top of his head in unseen vapors, but he managed to say that he would. He fell in beside the young woman, and they walked on together. To be so near the reality, the literal flesh and blood of what had been a long series of efflorescent dreams, quite stirred him. He gathered slowly, after each quick glance into the eyes which were not like those in the photograph; there they were set and did not resent his fancies; here they sparkled and talked and looked unutterable things at the helpless errant.

Miss Searles had been to a finishing school in the East, and either the school was a very good one or the little miss exceedingly apt, but both more probably true. She had the delicate pearls and peach-bloom on her cheeks to which the Western sun and winds are such persistent enemies, and a dear little nose tipped heavenward, as careless as a cat hunting its grandmother.

The rustle of her clothes mingled with little songs which the wind sang to the grass, a faint freshness of body with delicate spring-flower odors drifted to Ermine's active nostrils. But the eyes, the eyes, why did they not brood with him as in the picture? Why did they arch and laugh and tantalize?

His earthly senses had fled; gone somewhere else and left a riot in his blood. He tripped and stumbled, fell down, and crawled over answers to her questions, and he wished Lieutenant Butler was farther away than a pony could run in a week.

She stopped to raise her dress above the dusty road, and the scout overrode the alignment.

"Mr. Ermine, will you please carry my parasol for me?"

The object in question was newer to him than a man-of-war would have been. The prophet had explained about the great ships, but he had forgotten parasols. He did not exactly make out whether the thing was to keep the sun off, or to hide her face from his when she wanted to. He retraced his steps, wrapped his knuckles around the handle with a drowning clutch, and it burned his hand. If previously it had taken all his force to manœuvre himself, he felt now that he would bog down under this new weight. Atlas holding the world had a flying start of Ermine.

He raised it above her head, and she looked up at him so pleasantly, that he felt she realized his predicament; so he said, "Miss Searles, if I lug this baby tent into that scout camp, they will either shoot at us, or crawl the ponies and scatter out for miles. I think they would stand if you or the Lieutenant pack it; but if I do this, there won't be anything to see but ponies' tails wavering over the prairie."

"Oh, thank you; I will come to your rescue, Mr. Ermine." And she did.

"It is rather ridiculous, a parasol, but I do not intend to let the sun have its way with me." And glancing up, "Think if you had always carried a parasol, what a complexion you would have."

"But men don't carry them, do they?"

"Only when it rains; they do then, back in the States," she explained.

Ermine replied, "They do—hum!" and forthwith refused to consider men who did it.

"I think, Mr. Ermine, if I were an Indian, I should very much like to scalp you. I cannot cease to admire your hair."

"Oh, you don't have to be an Indian, to do that. Here is my knife; you can go ahead any time you wish," came the cheerful response.

"Mr. Butler, our friend succumbs easily to any fate at my hands, it seems. I wonder if he would let me eat him," said the girl.

"I will build the fire and put the kettle on for you." And Ermine was not joking in the least, though no one knew this.

They were getting into the dangerous open fields, and Miss Searles urged the scout in a different direction.

"Have you ever been East?"

"Yes," he replied, "I have been to Fort Buford."

The parasol came between them, and presently, "Would you like to go east of Buford—I mean away east of Buford," she explained.

"No; I don't want to go east or west, north or south of here," came the astonishing answer all in good faith, and Miss Searles mentally took to her heels. She feared seriousness.

"Oh, here are the Indians," she gasped, as they strode into the grotesque grouping. "I am afraid, Mr. Ermine—I know it is silly."

"What are you afraid of, Miss Searles?"

"I do not know; they look at me so!" And she gave a most delicious little shiver.

"You can't blame them for that; they're not made of wood." But this lost its force amid her peripatetic reflections.

"That's Broken-Shoe; that's White-Robe; that's Batailleur—oh, well, you don't care what their names are; you probably will not see them again."

"They are more imposing when mounted and dashing over the plains, I assure you. At a distance, one misses the details which rather obtrude here," ventured Butler.

"Very well; I prefer them where I am quite sure they will not dash. I very much prefer them sitting down quietly—such fearful-looking

"Will you please carry my parasol for me?"

faces. Oh my, they should be kept in cages like the animals in the Zoo. And do you have to fight such people, Mr. Butler?"

"We do," replied the officer, lighting a cigarette. This point of view was new and amusing.

One of the Indians approached the party. Ermine spoke to him in a loud, guttural, carrying voice, so different from his quiet use of English, that Miss Searles fairly jumped. The change of voice was like an explosion.

"Go back to your robe, brother; the white squaw is afraid of you—go back, I say!"

The intruder hesitated, stopped, and fastened Ermine with the vacant stare which in such times precede sudden, uncontrollable fury among Indians.

Again Ermine spoke: "Go back, you brown son of mules; this squaw is my friend; I tell you she is afraid of you. I am not. Go back, and before the sun is so high I will come to you. Make this boy go back, Broken-Shoe; he is a fool."

The old chieftain emitted a few hollow grunts, with a click between, and the young Indian turned away.

"My! Mr. Ermine, what are you saying? Have I offended the Indian? He looks daggers; let us retire—oh my, let us go—quick—quick!" And Ermine, by the flutter of wings, knew that his bird had flown. He followed, and in the safety of distance she lightly put her hand on his arm.

"What was it all about, Mr. Ermine? Do tell me."

Ermine's brain was not working on schedule time, but he fully realized what the affront to the Indian meant in the near future. He knew he would have to make his words good; but when the creature of his dreams was involved, he would have measured arms with a grizzly bear.

"He would not go back," said the scout, simply.

"But for what was he coming?" she asked.

"For you," was the reply.

"Goodness gracious! I had done nothing; did he want to kill me?"

"No, he wanted to shake hands with you; he is a fool."

"Oh, only to shake hands with me? And why did you not let him? I could have borne that."

"Because he is a fool," the scout ventured, and then in tones which carried the meaning, "Shake hands with you!"

"I see; I understand; you were protecting me; but he must hate you. I believe he will harm you; those dreadful Indians are so relentless, I have heard. Why did we ever go near the creatures? What will he do, Mr. Ermine?"

The scout cast his eye carefully up at the sky and satisfied the curiosity of both by drawling, "A—hu!"

"Well—well, Mr. Ermine, do not ever go near them again; I certainly would not if I were you. I shall see papa and have you removed from those ghastly beings. It is too dreadful. I have seen all I care to of them; let us go home, Mr. Butler."

The two—the young lady and the young man—bowed to Ermine, who touched the brim of his sombrero, after the fashion of the soldiers. They departed up the road, leaving Ermine to go, he knew not where, because he wanted to go only up the road. The abruptness of white civilities hashed the scout's contempt for time into fine bits; but he was left with something definite, at least, and that was a deep, venomous hatred for Lieutenant Butler; that was something he could hang his hat on. Then he thought of the "fool," and his footsteps boded ill for that one.

"That Ermine is such a tremendous man; do you not think so, Mr. Butler?"

"He seems a rather forceful person in his simple way," coincided the officer. "You apparently appeal to him strongly. He is downright romantic in his address, but I cannot find fault with the poor man. I am equally unfortunate."

"Oh, don't, Mr. Butler; I cannot stand it; you are, at least, sophisticated."

"Yes, I am sorry to say I am."

"Oh, please, Mr. Butler," with a deprecating wave of her parasol, "but tell me, aren't you afraid of them?"

"I suppose you mean the Indians. Well, they certainly earned my respect during the last campaign. They are the finest light-horse in the world, and if they were not encumbered with the women, herds, and villages; if they had plenty of ammunition and the buffalo would stay, I think there would be a great many army widows, Miss Searles."

"It is dreadful; I can scarcely remember my father; he has been made to live in this beast of a country since I was a child." Such was the lofty view the young woman took of her mundane progress.

"Shades of the vine-clad hills and citron groves of the Hudson River! I fear we brass buttoners are cut off. I should have been a lawyer or a priest—no, not a priest; for when I look at a pretty girl I cannot feel any priesthood in my veins."

Miss Searles whistled the bars of "Halt" from under the fortification of the parasol.

"Oh, well, what did the Lord make pretty women for?"

"I do not know, unless to demonstrate the foolishness of the line of Uncle Sam's cavalry," speculated the arch one. "Mr. Butler, if you do not stop, I shall run."

"All right; I am under arrest, so do not run; we are nearly home. I reserve my right to resume hostilities, however. I insist on fair play with your sagebrush admirer. Since we met in St. Louis, I have often wondered if we should ever see each other again. I always ardently wished we could."

"Mr. Butler, you are a poor imitation of our friend Ermine; he, at least, makes one feel that he means what he says," she rejoined.

"And you were good enough to remind me that I was sophisticated."

"I may have been mistaken," she observed. She played the batteries of her eyes on the unfortunate soldier, and all of his formations went down before them. He was in love, and she knew it, and he knew she knew it.

He felt like a fool, but tried not to act one, with the usual success of lovers. He was an easy victim of one of those greatest of natural weaknesses men have. She had him staked out and could bring him into her camp at any time the spirit moved her. Being a young person just from school, she found affairs easier than she had been led to suspect. In the usual girl way she had studied her casts, lures, and baits, but in reality they all seemed unnecessary, and she began to think some lethal weapon which would keep her admirers at a proper distance more to the purpose.

The handsome trooper was in no great danger, she felt, only she must have time; she did not want everything to happen in a minute, and the greatest dream of life vanish forever. Besides, she intended never, under any circumstances, to haul down her flag and surrender until after a good, hard siege.

They entered the cabin of the Searles, and there told the story of the morning's adventures. Mrs. Searles had the Indians classified with rattlesnakes, green devils, and hyenas, and expected scenes of this character to happen.

The Major wanted more details concerning Ermine. "Just what did he say, Butler?"

"I do not know; he spoke in some Indian language."

"Was he angry, and was the Indian who approached you mad?"

"They were like two dogs who stand ready to fight—teeth bared, muscles rigid, eyes set and just waiting for their nerves to snap," explained Butler.

"Oh, some d—— Indian row, no one knows what, and Ermine won't tell; yet as a rule these people are peaceful among themselves. I will ask him about it," observed the Major.

"Why can't you have Mr. Ermine removed from that awful scout camp, papa? Why can't he be brought up to some place near here? I do not see why such a beautiful white person as he is should have to associate with those savages," pleaded the graceful Katherine.

"Don't worry about Ermine, daughter; you wouldn't have him rank the Colonel out of quarters, would you? I will look into this matter a little."

Meanwhile the young scout walked rapidly toward his camp. He wanted to do something with his hands, something which would let the gathering electricity out at his finger-ends and relieve the strain, for the trend of events had irritated him.

Going straight to his tent, he picked up his rifle, loaded it, and buckled on the belt containing ammunition for it. He twisted his six-shooter round in front of him, and worked his knife up and down in its sheath. Then he strode out, going slowly down to the scout fire.

The day was warm; the white-hot sun cut traceries of the cotton-wood trees on the ground. A little curl of blue smoke rose straight upward from the fire, and in a wide ring of little groups sat or lounged the scouts. They seemingly paid no attention to the approach of Ermine, but one could not determine this; the fierce Western sun closes the eyelids in a perpetual squint, and leaves the beady eyes a chance to rove unobserved at a short distance.

Ermine came over and walked into the circle, stopping in front of the fire, thus facing the young Indian to whom he had used the harsh words. There was no sound except the rumble of a far-off government mule team and the lazy buzz of flies. He deliberately rolled a cigarette. Having done this to his satisfaction, he stooped down holding it against the coals, and it was ages before it caught fire. Then he put it to his lips, blew a cloud of smoke in the direction of his foe, and spoke in Absaroke.

"Well, I am here."

The silence continued; the Indian looked at him with a dull steady stare, but did nothing; finally Ermine withdrew. He understood; the Indian did not consider the time or opportunity propitious, but the scout did not flatter himself that such a time or place would never come. That was the one characteristic of an Indian of which a man could be certain.

CHAPTER FOURTEEN

In Love

John Ermine lay on his back in his tent, with one leg crossed over the other. His eyes were idly attracted by the play of shadows on the ducking, but his mind was visiting other places. He was profoundly discontented. During his life he had been at all times an easygoing person—taught in a rude school to endure embarrassing calamities and long-continued personal inconveniences by flood and hunger, bullets and snow. He had no conception of the civilized trait of acquisitiveness whereby he had escaped that tantalization. He desired military distinction, but he had gotten that. No man strode the camp whose deeds were better recognized than his, not even the Colonel commanding.

His attitude toward mankind had always been patient and kindly except when urged into other channels by war. He even had schooled himself to the irksome labor at the prophet's mine, low delving which seemed useless; and had acquiesced while Crooked-Bear stuffed his head with the thousand details of white mentality; but now vaguely he began to feel a lack of something, an effort which he had not made—a something he had left undone; a difference and a distinction between himself and the officers who were so free to associate with the creature who had borrowed his mind and given nothing in return. No one in the rude campaigning which had been the lot of all since he joined had made any noticeable social distinction toward him—rather otherwise; they had sought and trusted him, and more than that, he had been singled out for special good will. He was free to call at any officer's quarters on the line, sure of a favorable reception; then why did he not go to Major Searles'? At the thought he lay heavier on the blanket, and dared not trust his legs to carry out his inclinations.

The camp was full of fine young officers who would trust their legs and risk their hearts—he felt sure of that. True, he was subject to the orders of certain officials, but so were they. Young officers had asked him to do favors on many occasions, and he did them, because it was clear that they ought to be done, and he also had explained devious plains-craft to them of which they had instantly availed themselves. The arrangement was natural and not oppressive.

Captain Lewis could command him to ford a rushing torrent: could tell him to stand on his head and be d—— quick about it, and of course he would do anything for him and Major Searles; they could ask nothing which the thinker would not do in a lope. As for Colonel Miles, the fine-looking man who led "ten thousand" in the great white battles, it was a distinction to do exactly what he ordered—every one did that; then why did he not go to Major Searles' quarters, he kept asking himself. He was not afraid of Colonel Miles or Captain Lewis or Major Searles or any officer, but—and the thought flashed, he was wary of the living eyes of the beloved photograph. Before these he could not use his mind, hands, or feet; his nerves shivered like aspen leaves in a wind, and the blood surged into his head until he could see nothing with his eyes; cold chills played up and down his spine; his hair crawled round under his sombrero, and he was most thoroughly miserable, but some way he no longer felt contentment except while undergoing this misery.

He lay on the blanket while his thoughts alternately fevered and chilled his brain. So intense were his emotions that they did more than disorder his mind: they took smart hold of his very body, gnawing and constricting his vitals until he groaned aloud.

No wild beast which roamed the hills was less conscious, ordinarily, of its bodily functions than Ermine. The machinery of a perfect physique had always responded to the vital principle and unwound to the steady pull of the spring of life, yet he found himself now stricken. It was not a thing for the surgeon, and he gradually gave way before its steady progress. His nature was a rich soil for the seeds of idealism which warm imagination constantly sprinkled, and the fruits became a consuming passion.

His thoughts were burning him. Getting up from his bed, he took a kettle and small axe, saddled his pony, and took himself off toward the river. As he rode along he heard the Englishman call out to him, but he did not answer. The pony trotted away, leaving the camp far behind, until he suddenly came to a little prairie surrounded by cottonwoods, in the middle of which were numbers of small wick-e-ups made by the Indians for sweat-baths. He placed his blankets and ponchos over one, made a fire and heated a number of rocks, divested himself of his clothing, and taking his pail of water got inside, crouching while he dashed handfuls of water over the hot rocks. This simple remedy would do more than cleanse the skin and was always resorted to for common ills by the Indians. After Ermine came out he plunged into the cold waters of the Yellowstone and dressed himself, but he did not feel any better. He mounted and rode off, forgetting his axe, blankets, and pail; such furnishings were unconsidered now. In response to a tremendous desire to do something, he ran his pony for a mile, but that did not calm the yearning.

"I feel like a piece of fly blown meat," he said to himself. "I think I will go to Saw-Bones and let him have a hack at me; I never was so sick before." And to the cabin of the surgeon he betook himself.

That gentleman was fussing about with affairs of his own, when Ermine entered.

"Say, doctor, give me some medicine."

"What's the matter with you?" asked the addressed, shoving his sombrero to one side and looking up incredulously.

"Oh, I'm sick."

"Well, where are you sick?"

Ermine brushed his hair from off his forehead, slapped his leggings with his quirt, and answered, "Sick all over—kind of low fever, like a man with a bullet in him."

"Bilious, probably." And the doctor felt his pulse and looked into his bright, clear eyes.

"Oh, nonsense, boy—you are not sick. I guess loafing around is bad for you. The Colonel ought to give you a hundred miles with his compliments to some one; but here is a pill which will cure you." Saying which, the physician brought out his box containing wheat bread rolled into small balls, that he always administered to cases which he did not understand or to patients whom he suspected of shirking on "sick report."

Ermine swallowed it and departed.

The doctor tipped his sombrero forward and laughed aloud in long, cadenced peals as he sorted his vials.

"Sick!" he muttered; "funny—funny—funny sick! One could not kill him with an axe. I guess he is sick of sitting round—sick to be loping over the wild plains. Humph—sick!"

Ermine rode down the officers' row, but no one was to be seen. He pulled his horse's head up before Major Searles' door, but instantly slapped him with his whip and trotted on to his tent.

"If that fool Indian boy would only show himself," he thought; but the Indian was not a fool, and did not. Again Ermine found himself lying on his back, more discontented than ever. The day waned and the shadows on the tent walls died, but still he lay. Ramon stuck his head in at the flaps.

"Well—ah got your British man hees pony, Ermine—trade twenty-five dollar in goods for five pony."

"Oh, d—— the Englishman," was the response to this, whereat Ramon took a good long stare at his friend and withdrew. He failed to understand the abruptness, and went away wondering how Ermine could know that he had gouged Mr. Harding a little on the trade. Still this did not explain; for he had confidence in his own method of blinding his trail. He was a business man and a moral cripple.

The sun left the world and Ermine with his gloomy thoughts.

*   *   *   *   *   *

Late at night Captain Lewis sat at his desk writing letters, the lamp spotting on the white disk of his hat, which shaded his face, while the pale moonlight crept in through the open door. A sword clanked outside, and with a knock the officer of the guard hurriedly entered.

"Say, Bill, I have your scout Ermine down by the guard house, and he's drunk. I didn't lock him up. Wanted to see you first. If I lock him up, I am afraid he'll pull out on you when he comes to. What shall I do?"

"The devil you say—Ermine drunk? Why, I never knew him to drink; it was a matter of principle with him; often told me that his mentor, whoever he was, told him not to."

"Well, he's drunk now, so there you are," said the officer.

"How drunk?"

"Oh, good and drunk."

"Can he walk?" Lewis queried.

"No; all he can do is lay on his back and shoot pretty thick Injun at the moon."

"Does every one know of this?"

"No; Corporal Riley and Private Bass of Company K brought him up from Wilmore's whiskey-shack, and they are sitting on his chest out back of the guard house. Come on," spoke the responsible one.

Lewis jumped up and followed. They quickly made their way to the spot, and there Lewis beheld Ermine lying on his back. The moonlight cut his fine face softly and made the aureole of his light hair stand away from the ground. He moaned feebly, but his eyes were closed. Corporal Riley and Private Bass squatted at his head and feet with their eyes fastened on the insensible figure. Off to one side a small pile of Ermine's lethal weapons shimmered. The post was asleep; a dog barked, and an occasional cow-bell tinkled faintly down in the quarter-master's corral.

"Gad!" gasped Lewis, as he too stooped down. "How did this happen, Corporal?"

"Well, I suppose we might as well tell it as it is," Bass replied, indirectly conscious of the loyalty he owed his brother sinner. "We ran the guard, sir, and went down to Wilmore's, and when we got there, we found this feller pretty far gone with drink. He had his guns out, and was talking Injun, and he had Wilmore hiding out in the sagebrush. I beefed him under the ear, and we took his guns away, sir. I didn't hurt him much; he was easy money with his load, and then we packed him up here, and I told the officer of the guard, sir."

"Well," said Lewis, finally, "make a chair of your hands and bring him down to my quarters."

The soldiers gathered up the limp form, while Lewis took the belt and pistols.

"No use of reporting this?"

"No," answered the officer of the guard.

The men laid him out on the Captain's bed after partially disrobing him, and started to withdraw.

"Go to your quarters, men, and keep your mouths shut; you will understand it is best for you."

The two saluted and passed out, leaving the Captain pacing the floor, and groping wildly for an explanation.

"Why, I have offered that boy a drink out of my own flask on campaign, when we were cold enough and tired enough to make my old Aunt Jane weaken on her blue ribbon; but he never did. That was good of the men to bring him in, and smart of Welbote not to chuck him in the guard house. Sailor's sins! He'd never stand that; it would kill his pride, and he has pride, this long-haired wild boy. He may tell me in the morning, but I am not so sure of that. Laying down on his luck is not the way he plays it. I don't doubt it was an accident, and maybe it will teach him a d—— good lesson; he'll have a head like a hornets' nest tomorrow morning."

The Captain, after a struggle with the strange incident, sought his couch, and when he arose next morning betook himself to Ermine's room. He found him asleep amid the tangle of his wonderful hair, and he smiled as he pictured the scout's surprise when he awoke; in fact, he pulled himself together for a little amusement. A few remarks to reënforce the headache would do more good than a long brief without a big "exhibit A," such as would accompany the awakening.

The steady gaze of the Captain awoke the scout, and he opened his eyes, which wandered about the room, but displayed no interest; they set themselves on the Captain's form, but refused to believe these dreams, and closed again. The Captain grinned and addressed the empty room:

"How would you like to be a millionnaire and have that headache? Oh, gee—'twould bust a mule's skull."

The eyes opened again and took more account of things; they began to credit their surroundings. When the scene had assembled itself, Ermine sat up on the bed, saying, "Where am I? What hit me?" and then he lay down again. His dream had come true; he was sick.

"You are in my bed, so stay there, and you will come out all right. You have been making the Big Red Medicine; the devil is pulling your hair, and every time he yanks, he will say, 'John Ermine, don't do that again.' Keep quiet, and you will get well." After saying which Lewis left the room.

All day long the young man lay on the bed; he was burning at the stake; he was being torn apart by wild horses; the regimental band played its bangiest music in his head; the big brass drum would nearly blow it apart; and his poor stomach kept trying to crawl out of his body in its desperate strife to escape Wilmore's decoction of high-wine. This lasted all day, but by evening the volcano had blown itself out, when a natural sleep overcame him.

Captain Lewis had the knowledge of certain magic, well enough known in the army, to alleviate Ermine's condition somewhat, but he chose not to use it; he wanted "exhibit A" to wind up in a storm of fireworks.

As Ermine started out the next morning Lewis called, "Hey, boy, how did you come to do it?"

Ermine turned a half-defiant and half-questioning front to Lewis and tossed his matted hair. "I don't know, Captain; it all seems as though I must have fallen off the earth; but I'm back now and think I can stay here."

"Well, no one knows about it except myself, so don't say a word to any one, and don't do it again—sabe?"

"You bet I won't. If the soldiers call that drowning their sorrows, I would rather get along with mine."

CHAPTER FIFTEEN

BRINGING IN THE WOLF

"Going to follow the dogs today, Lewis?" said Lieutenant Shockley, poking his head in the half-open door.

"Yes, reckon I'll give this chair a vacation; wait a minute," and he mauled the contents of his ditty-box after the manner of men and bears when in search of trifles. A vigorous stirring is bound to upheave what is searched for, so in due course the Captain dug up a snaffle-bit.

"I find my horse goes against this better than the government thing—when the idea is to get there and d—— formations."

"Well, shake yourself, Lewis; the people are pulling out."

"What, ahead of the scouts?" laughed the chief of them.

"Yes; and you know the line never retires on the scouts; so smoke up."

The orderly having changed the bits, the two mounted and walked away. "'Spose this is for the Englishman. Great people these Englishmen—go trotting all over the earth to chase something; anything will do from rabbits to tigers, and niggers preferred," said Lewis.

"Must be a great deprivation to most Englishmen to have to live in England where there is nothing to chase. I suppose they all have this desire to kill something; a great hardship it must be," suggested Shockley.

"Oh, I think they manage," continued Lewis; "from what I understand the rich and the great go batting about the globe after heads; the so-so fellows go into the army and navy to take their chance of a killing, and the lower orders have to find contentment in staying at home, where there is no amusement but pounding each other."

"There goes your friend Ermine on that war-pony of his; well, he can show his tail to any horse in cantonments. By the way, some one was telling me that he carries a medicine-bag with him; isn't he a Christian?"

"Oh, I don't know. He reminds me of old Major Doyle of ours, who was promoted out of us during the war, but who rejoined in Kansas and was retired. You don't remember him? He was an Irishman and a Catholic; he had been in the old army since the memory of man runneth not to the contrary, and ploughed his way up and down all over the continent. And there was Major Dunham—you know him. He and Doyle had been comrades since youth; they had fought and marched together, spilled many a noggin in each other's honor, and who drew the other's monthly pay depended on the paste-boards. Old Doyle came into post, one day, and had a lot of drinks with the fellows as he picked up the social threads. Finally he asked: 'Un' phware is me ole friend, Dunham? Why doesn't he come down and greet me with a glass?'

"Some one explained that old Dunham had since married, had joined the church, and didn't greet any one over glasses any more.

"'Un' phwat church did he join?'

"Some one answered, the Universalist Church.

"'Ah, I see,' said Doyle, tossing off his drink, 'he's huntin' an aisy ford.' So I guess that's what Ermine is doing."

They soon joined the group of mounted officers and ladies, orderlies, and nondescripts of the camp, all alive with anticipations, and their horses stepping high.

"Good morning, Mr. Harding; how do you find yourself?" called out Captain Lewis.

"Fine—fine, thank you."

"How are you mounted?"

Harding patted his horse's neck, saying: "Quite well—a good beast; seems to manage my weight, but I find this saddle odd. Bless me, I know there is no habit in the world so strong as the saddle. I have the flat saddle habit."

"What we call a rim-fire saddle," laughed Searles, who joined the conversation.

"Ah—a rim-fire, do you call them? Well, do you know, Major, I should say this saddle was better adapted to carrying a sack of corn than a man," rejoined Harding.

"Oh, you'll get along; there isn't a fence nearer than St. Paul except the quartermaster's corral."

"I say, Searles," spoke Lewis, "there's the Colonel out in front—happy as a boy out of school; glad there's something to keep him quiet; we must do this for him every day, or he'll have us out pounding sagebrush."

"And there's the quartermaster with a new popper on his whip," sang some voice.

"There is no champagne like the air of the high plains before the sun burns the bubble out of it," proclaimed Shockley, who was young and without any of the saddle or collar marks of life; "and to see these beautiful women riding along—say, Harding, if I get off this horse I'll set this prairie on fire," and he burst into an old song:

> Now, ladies, good-by to each kind, gentle soul,
> Though me coat it is ragged, me heart it is whole;
> There's one sitting yonder I think wants a beau,
> Let her come to the arms of young Billy Barlow.

And Shockley urged his horse to the side of Miss Katherine Searles.

Observing the manœuvre, Captain Lewis poked her father in the ribs. "I don't think your daughter wants a beau very much, Major; the youngsters are four files deep around her now."

"'Tis youth, Bill Lewis; we've all had it once, and from what I observe, they handle it pretty much as we used to."

"The very same. I don't see how men write novels or plays about that old story; all they can do is to invent new fortifications for Mr. Hero to carry before she names the day."

Lieutenant Shockley found himself unable to get nearer than two horses to Miss Searles, so he bawled: "And I thought you fellows

Shockley

were hunting wolves. I say, Miss Searles, if you ride one way and the wolf runs the other, it is easy to see which will have the larger field. My money is on you—two to one. Who will take the wolf?"

"Oh, Mr. Shockley, between you and this Western sun, I shall soon need a new powder puff."

"Shall I challenge him?" called Bowles to the young woman.

"Please not, Mr. Bowles; I do not want to lose him." And every one greeted Shockley derisively.

"Guide right!" shouted the last, putting his horse into a lope. Miss Searles playfully slashed about with her riding-whip, saying, "Deploy, gentlemen," and followed him. The others broke apart; they had been beaten by the strategy of the loud mouth. Lieutenant Butler, however, permitted himself the pleasure of accompanying Miss Searles; his determination could not be shaken by these diversions; he pressed resolutely on.

"I think Butler has been hit over the heart," said one of the dispersed cavaliers.

"You bet, and it is a disabling wound too. I wonder if Miss Searles intends to cure him. When I see her handle her eyes, methinks, compadre, she's a cruel little puss. I wouldn't care to be her mouse."

"But, fellows, she's pretty, a d—— pretty girl, hey!" ventured a serious youngster. "You can bet any chap here would hang out the white flag and come a-running, if she hailed him."

And so, one with another, they kept the sacred fire alight. As for that matter, the aforesaid Miss Puss knew how her men valued the difficulties of approach, which was why she scattered them. She proposed to take them in detail. Men do not weaken readily before each other, but alone they are helpless creatures, when the woman understands herself. She can then sew them up, tag them, and put them away on various shelves, and rely on them to stay there; but it requires management, of course.

"I say, Miss Searles, those fellows will set spring guns and bear traps for me tonight; they will never forgive me."

"Oh, well, Mr. Shockley, to be serious, I don't care. Do you suppose a wolf will be found? I am so bored." Which remark caused the eminent Lieutenant to open his mouth very wide in imitation of a laugh, divested of all mirth.

"Miss Katherine Searles," he said, in mock majesty, "I shall do myself the honor to crawl into the first badger-hole we come to and stay there until you dig me out."

"Don't be absurd; you know I always bury my dead. Mr. Butler, do you expect we shall find a wolf? Ah, there is that King Charles cavalier, Mr. Ermine—for all the world as though he had stepped from an old frame. I do think he is lovely."

"Oh, bother that yellow Indian; he is such a nuisance," jerked Butler.

"Why do you say that? I find him perfectly new; he never bores me, and he stood between me and that enraged savage."

"A regular play. I do not doubt he arranged it beforehand. However, it was well thought out—downright dramatic, except that the Indian ought to have killed him."

"Oh, would you have arranged it that way if you had been playwright?"

"Yes," replied the bilious lover.

Shaking her bridle rein, she cried, "Come, Mr. Shockley, let us ride to Ermine; at least you will admire him." Shockley enjoyed the death stroke which she had administered to Butler, but saying to himself as he thought of Ermine, "D—— the curly boy," and followed his charming and difficult quarry. He alone had ridden true.

The independent and close-lipped scout was riding outside the group. He never grew accustomed to the heavy columns, and did not talk on the march—a common habit of desert wanderers. But his eye covered everything. Not a buckle or a horsehair or the turn of a leg escaped him, and you may be sure Miss Katherine Searles was detailed in his picture.

He had beheld her surrounded by the young officers until he began to hate the whole United States army. Then he saw her dismiss the escort saving only two, and presently she reduced her force to one. As she came toward him, his blood took a pop into his head, which helped mightily to illumine his natural richness of color. She was really coming to him. He wished it, he wanted it, as badly as a man dying of thirst wants water, and yet a whole volley of bullets would not disturb him as her coming did.

"Good morning, Mr. Ermine; you, too, are out after wolves, I see," sang Katherine, cheerily.

"No, ma'm, I don't care anything about wolves; and why should I care for them?"

"What are you out for then, pray?"

"Oh, I don't know; thought I would like to see you after wolves. I guess that's why I am out," came the simple answer.

"Well, to judge by the past few miles I don't think you will see me after them today."

"I think so myself, Miss Searles. These people ought to go back in the breaks of the land to find wolves; they don't give a wolf credit for having eyes."

"Why don't you tell them so, Mr. Ermine?" pleaded the young woman.

"The officers think they know where to find them; they would not thank me, and there might not be anywhere I would go to find them. It does not matter whether we get one or none, anyhow," came Ermine's sageness.

"Indeed, it does matter. I must have a wolf."

"Want him alive or dead?" was the low question.

"What! Am I to have one?"

"You are," replied the scout, simply.

"When?"

"Well, Miss Searles, I can't order one from the quartermaster exactly, but if you are in a great hurry, I might go now."

"Mr. Ermine, you will surely kill me with your generosity. You have offered me your scalp, your body, and now a wolf. Oh, by the way, what did that awful Indian say to you? I suppose you have seen him since."

"Didn't say anything."

"Well, I hope he has forgiven you; but as I understand them, that is not the usual way among Indians."

"No, Miss Searles, he won't forgive me. I'm a-keeping him to remember you by."

"How foolish; I might give you something for a keepsake which would leave better memories, do you not think so?"

"You might, if you wish to."

The girl was visibly agitated at this, coming as it did from her crude admirer. She fumbled about her dress, her hair, and finally drew off her glove and gave it to the scout, with a smile so sweet and a glance of the eye which penetrated Ermine like a charge of buckshot. He took the glove and put it inside of the breast of his shirt, and said, "I'll get the wolf."

Shockley was so impressed with the conversation that he was surprised into silence, and to accomplish that phenomenon took a most powerful jolt, as every one in the regiment knew. He could talk the bottom out of a nose-bag, or put a clock to sleep. Ordinary verbal jollity did not seem at all adequate, so he carolled a passing line:

One little, two little, three little Injuns,
Four little, five little, six little Injuns,
Seven little, eight little, nine little Injuns,
　　　Ten little Injun boys.

This came as an expiring burst which unsettled his horse though it relieved him. Shockley needed this much yeast before he could rise again.

"Oh, Mr. Shockley, you must know Mr. Ermine."

"I have the pleasure, Miss Searles; haven't I, Ermine?"

The scout nodded assent.

"We were side by side when we rushed the point of that hill in the Sitting Bull fight last fall; remember that, Ermine?"

"Yes, sir," said the scout; but the remembrance evidently did not cause Ermine's E string to vibrate. Fighting was easier, freer; but altogether it was like washing the dishes at home compared with the dangers which now beset him.

Suddenly every one was whipping and spurring forward; the pack of greyhounds were streaking it for the hills. "Come on," yelled Shockley, "here's a run." And that mercurial young man's scales tipped right readily from his heart to his spurs.

"It's only a coyote, Miss Searles," said Ermine; but the young woman spatted her horse with her whip and rode bravely after the flying Shockley. Ermine's fast pony kept steadily along with her under a pull; the plainsman's long, easy sway in the saddle was unconscious, and he never took his eyes from the girl, now quite another person under the excitement.

Every one in the hunting-party was pumping away to the last ounce. A pack of greyhounds make a coyote save all the time he can; they stimulate his interest in life, and those who have seen a good healthy specimen burn up the ground fully realize the value of passing moments.

"Oh, dear; my hat is falling off!" shrieked the girl.

"Shall I save it, Miss Searles?"

"Yes! Yes! Catch it!" she screamed.

Ermine brought his flying pony nearer hers on the off side and reached his hand toward the flapping hat, struggling at a frail anchorage of one hat-pin, but his arm grew nerveless at the near approach to divinity.

"Save it! Save it!" she called.

"Shall I?" and he pulled himself together.

Dropping his bridle-rein over the pommel of his saddle, standing in his stirrups as steadily as a man in church, he undid the hat with both hands. When he had released it and handed it to its owner, she heard him mutter hoarsely, "My God!"

"Oh, Mr. Ermine, I hope the pin did not prick you."

"No, it wasn't the pin."

"Ah," she ejaculated barely loud enough for him to hear amid the rushing hoof-beats.

The poor man was in earnest, and the idea drove the horses, the hounds, and the coyote out of her mind, and she ran her mount harder than ever. She detested earnest men, having so far in her career with the exception of Mr. Butler found them great bores; but drive as she would, the scout pattered at her side, and she dared not look at him.

These two were by no means near the head of the drive, as the girl's horse was a stager, which had been selected because he was highly educated concerning badger-holes and rocky hillsides.

Orderlies clattered behind them, and Private Patrick O'Dowd and Private Thompson drew long winks at each other.

"Oi do be thinkin' the long bie's harse cud roon fasther eff the divil was afther him. Faith, who'd roon away from a fairy?"

"The horse is running as fast as is wanted," said Thompson, sticking his hooks into the Indian pony which he rode.

"Did yez obsarve the bie ramove the hat from the lady, and his pony shootin' gravel into our eyes fit to smother?" shouted O'Dowd, using the flat of his hand as a sounding-board to Thompson.

"You bet, Pat; and keeping the gait he could take a shoe off her horse, if she wanted it done."

"They say seein's believin', but Oi'll not be afther tellin' the story in quarters. Oi'm eaight year in the ahrmy, and Oi can lie whin it's convanient."

The dogs overhauled the unfortunate little wolf despite its gallant efforts, and it came out of the snarling mass, as some wag had expressed it, "like a hog going to war—in small pieces." The field closed up and dismounted, soldier fashion, at the halt.

"What's the matter with the pony today, Ermine? Expected you'd be ahead of the wolf at least," sang out Lewis.

"I stopped to pick up a hat," he explained; but Captain Lewis fixed his calculating eye on his man and bit his mustache. Events had begun to arrange themselves; that drunken night and Ermine's apathy toward the Englishman's hunting-party—and he had stopped to pick up her hat—oho!

Without a word the scout regained his seat and loped away toward the post, and Lewis watched him for some time, in a brown study; but a man of his years often fails to give the ardor of youth its proper value, so his mind soon followed more natural thoughts.

"Your horse is not a very rapid animal, I observe, Miss Searles," spoke Butler.

"Did you observe that? I did not notice that you were watching me, Mr. Butler."

"Oh, I must explain that in an affair of this kind I am expected to sustain the reputation of the cavalry. I forced myself to the front."

"Quite right. I kept the only man in the rear, who was capable of spoiling your reputation; you are under obligations to me."

"That wild man, you mean. He certainly has a wonderful pony, but you need not trouble about him if it is to please me only."

"I find this sun becoming too insistent; I think I will go back," said Katherine Searles. Many of the women also turned their horses homeward, leaving only the more pronounced types of sportsmen to search for another wolf.

"Having sustained the cavalry, I'll accompany you, Katherine."

"Miss Searles, please!" she said, turning to him, and the little gem of a nose asserted itself.

"Oh, dear me! What have I done? You permitted me to call you Katherine only last night."

"Yes, but I do not propose to divide my friendship with a nasty little gray wolf which has been eaten up alive."

The officer ran his gauntlet over his eyes.

"I am such a booby. I see my mistake, Miss Searles, but the idea you advance seems so ridiculous—to compare yourself with a wolf."

"Oh, I say, Miss Searles," said Shockley, riding up, "may I offer you one of my gauntlets? The sun, I fear, will blister your bare hand."

"No, indeed." And Butler tore off a glove, forcing it into her hand. She could not deny him, and pulled it on. "Thank you; I lost one of mine this morning."

Then she turned her eyes on Mr. Shockley with a hard little expression, which sealed him up. He was prompt to feel that the challenge meant war, and war with this girl was the far-away swing of that gallant strategic pendulum.

"Yes," Shockley added, "one is apt to drop things without noting them, in a fast rush. I dropped something myself this morning."

"Pray what was it, Mr. Shockley?"

"It was an idea," he replied with a shrug of the shoulders.

"An idea?" laughed she, appreciating Shockley's discretion. "I hope you have more of them than I have gloves."

"I have only one," he sighed.

"Are all soldiers as stupid as you are, my dear sir?"

"All under thirty, I am sorry to say," and this from Shockley too. Miss Searles applied the whip; but go as she would, the two officers did not lose again the idea, but kept their places beside her.

"You are not very steady under fire," laughed Shockley.

"You are such an absurd person."

"I may be a blessing in disguise."

"You may be; I am unable to identify you."

"The chaperon is waving her whip at us, Miss Searles," cautioned Butler.

"Private O'Dowd is my chaperon, and he can stand the pace," she replied.

The young woman drove on, leaving a pall of dust behind, until the little party made the cantonment and drew rein in front of the Searleses' quarters. Giving her hand to the orderly, she dismissed her escort and disappeared.

"Well, Katherine," said Mrs. Searles, "did you enjoy your ride?"

"Yes, mother, but my horse is such an old poke I was nowhere in the race."

"The Major says he is a safe horse; one which can be relied on, and that is more important than speed. I do not want your neck broken, my dear."

"Neither do I want my neck broken, but I should like to be somewhere in sight during a run. The young officers desert me once a wolf is sighted; they forget their manners at the first flash of a greyhound."

"I know, daughter, but what can you expect? They go out for that purpose."

"Mr. Ermine doesn't, or at least he is polite enough to say that he goes out to see me run, and not the wolf. If he is not sophisticated, he seems to have the primitive instincts of a gentleman."

"Mr. Ermine, forsooth!" And Madam Searles betrayed some asperity. "Is he presumptuous enough to present you with compliments? You had better maintain your distance."

"He is a perfectly delightful man, mother; so thoughtful and so handsome."

"Tut tut, Katherine; he is only an ordinary scout—a wild man."

"I don't care; I like him."

"Katherine, what are you thinking of?"

"Oh, I don't know, mother; I am thinking what an absurd lot men are. They insist on talking nonsense at me. They do not seem to preserve their reserve; they are not a bit like the men back in the States."

"Well, my daughter, you must be careful not to provoke familiarity. Young women are rather scarce out here, and you are not without your charms. I believe you use your eyes more than you should. Have a care; do not forget that quiet modesty is the most becoming thing in the world for a woman."

"I am sure I do nothing; in fact, I have to be constantly menacing these military youths to keep them from coming too near, especially Mr. Shockley and Mr. Butler. I am in distress every minute for fear Mr. Butler will say more than I am ready to hear."

Mrs. Searles was by no means averse to Butler's attentions to her daughter. "A very fine young man," was her comment when she thought of him. Both women knew that the Lieutenant was ready to draw his sabre in Katherine's behalf.

Katherine had met Butler while visiting St. Louis the year before, had come to know him well, and didn't pretend to dislike him. His father and mother were dead, but his people were of consequence.

Mrs. Searles determined to ask the Major to make some inquiries about her daughter's suitor, and meanwhile dismissed Katherine with the caution not to tempt this midday sun overmuch; "It will soon turn your peach-blow into russet apples," she told her, "and men, you know, like the peach-blow. Without it you might be less troubled by the young officers."

*　　　*　　　*　　　*　　　*　　　*

The sun was about to depart. The families of the officers were sitting under their *ramadas* enjoying the cool. Butler and Shockley with two or three other men were seated with the Searleses when their attention was attracted by a commotion down by the quarters.

"What's the circus?"

"Don't make out; seems to be coming this way. It is—why, it is the scout Ermine!"

The group sat expectantly and witnessed the approach of John Ermine on his horse. At some distance to one side rode Wolf-Voice, and gradually through the dusk they made out some small animal between them—a dog-like thing.

The riders drew up before the Searleses' hut, and every one rose. The object was a scared and demoralized wolf with his tail between his legs. His neck was encircled by two rawhide lariats which ran to the pommels of the riders.

Touching his hat, Ermine said, "Miss Searles, I have brought you the wolf."

"Goodness gracious, Mr. Ermine! I only said that in fun. What can I possibly do with a wolf?"

"I don't know. You said you wanted one, so here he is."

"Yaes," said Wolf-Voice, with an oath, "she was bite my harm hoff; you no want heem; I skin her alive." He had previously warned Ermine that no one but a d—— fool would want a live wolf.

"Well, daughter, what are you going to do with it? Start a Zoo? I don't know where we can put him," spoke Major Searles, in perplexity.

"He will have to roost high if the dogs find out about this visitation," observed Shockley.

"How did you get him, Ermine?"

"Dug him out of his den, and before we got him roped he pinched Wolf-Voice, and I had a hard time to keep him from killing the beast."

"Yaes; no want him, an' we dig a hole mile deep mabeso—dig ever since sun she so high, ten-as tol-a-pas." And in his disgust Wolf-Voice was about to slacken his rope.

"Hold up there; don't turn that animal loose near here! Take him down to the corral and lock him up. We'll see tomorrow what can be done with him," spoke Searles.

Ermine and Wolf-Voice turned and drifted out into the gathering darkness with their forlorn tow, while a few soldiers with clubs fought the dogs off as they gradually began to gather around their natural enemy.

"Why, I only asked for a wolf in the most casual way—in a joking way; you heard me, Mr. Shockley."

"Yes, I did hear you, but I also heard him say you should have one, and I thought at the time he looked serious about it."

"I was so astonished that I did not properly thank him," she added; "and the Indian was in a lovely humor over the whole episode; his disgust was most apparent. I must be more careful what I say to Mr. Ermine."

"I have it," cried the Major; "we'll make up a purse, buy the wolf, and run him so soon as he gets over the effects of his capture."

"No, no, papa, you must not offend Ermine with money. He would be awfully offended; that would be the very last thing to do to him."

CHAPTER SIXTEEN

A HUNT

TROOP OF CAVALRY TROTTED ALONG through the early morning dust, and Lieutenant Butler drew out at the Searleses' quarters, tying his horse for a moment in front, while he went inside. It was early for casual people. He did not stay long, but the sergeant in the rear thought he saw a girl come to the door and kiss him good-by. As the officer dashed to the head of the troop, the old sergeant dipped a smiling countenance deep into a plug of tobacco.

"Hello! There goes Butler with his troop," said Mr. Harding to Captain Lewis, as they basked in the morning sun before that officer's quarters.

"Yes, he goes to escort some wagons; but the fact is, internecine war has broken out in the post, and he goes for the good of the service. It's all about a damn little yellow dog."

"A dog make a war! How, pray?"

"Oh gee! Yes! Dogs and rum and women make all the trouble there is in the army, and particularly dogs. That sounds odd, doesn't it? Nevertheless, it's a hard, dry fact. Soldiers take to dogs, and it's always 'kick my dog kick me' with these bucks. That troop has a miserable runt of a *fice,* and he's smart the same as such pups often are. The cavalrymen have taught him to nip at infantrymen, which they think is great fun. Some of the infantrymen got tired of sewing up three-cornered tears in their galligaskins and allowed they would assassinate said *fice*. Here is where these baby cavalrymen lose their temper and threaten to fire on the company-quarters of any outfit which bags Fido—and that's war. It has been fixed up. Some officer has arranged an armistice, and meanwhile the troop gets a few miles in the sage-brush, which, it is hoped, will be credited to the pup, whereat he won't be so popular."

"Ah, a very sad case for the doggie," added Harding; "he was taught to take wrong views of the service."

"Let us go down and take a look at Ermine's wolf," said Lewis, and the two proceeded to the quartermaster's corral, where they found a group standing about the wolf.

It was held by a stout chain and lay flat on the ground, displaying an entire apathy concerning the surroundings, except that it looked "Injuny," as a passing mule-skinner observed.

"When I see one of those boys, it makes my back come up like a cat's," said Lewis. "A bunch of them nearly pulled me down two years ago on the Canadian. I fired all my ammunition at them and got into camp just about the right time; a half a mile more and I would have got my 'final statement.'"

"Yes, I have hunted them in Poland, on moonlight nights. A wolf in the deep forests on a moonlight night harmonizes better than one tied by a chain, with twenty men staring at him in broad daylight."

An irrepressible private shoved his nose into the circle, looked at the captive, and departed saying:

He enlisted in the army,
　　The bullets took their toll,
The wolves got his body,
　　And the divil got his soul.
　　　　Om-a yah-ha-ha.

Poor wolf! He possessed too many attributes of man to ingratiate himself. He did not admit their superiority, and lay stoically under the heel of the conqueror; all thumbs were down for him.

He was apostrophized by a soldier: "Ah, me innocent-lukin' child of the divil—wait till ye git thim hoop-shnake dawgs afther yez."

Major Searles rode in through the gate and sang out: "The Colonel has a few papers to sign, after which he says we will chase the wolf; so you can get ready, gentlemen, those who care to run." And then to Ermine, who stood near: "Miss Searles thinks that will be a proper disposition of your valuable present. Can you manage to turn him loose?"

"Why, yes, I suppose we can. Putting the ropes on him is easier than taking them off. I won't take him out until you are all ready; every dog in the camp will fly at him. Can I have four or five soldiers to drive them off? Wolf-Voice and myself will be on horseback, and can't protect him."

"Certainly, certainly!" And under the Major's directions various soldiers armed themselves with whips, and undertook to make a rear-guard fight with the garrison pups.

Horses were saddled, and went clattering to all points of the post. The certainty of a run drew every one out. Shockley aided Miss Searles to mount, saying, "I am on duty today; my thoughts will fly where my pony should. You cannot doubt where he would go."

"Poor man, do not look so woebegone; it does not become you. I like you better when you sing than when you cry."

"If you didn't make me cry, I should sing all the time."

"Oh, that would be bad for your voice, my dear Mr. Shockley, as we say on a letter head." And she mocked him beyond her rapier point, as she rode along, followed by the rapidly receding words:

Don't forget me, Molly darling;
    Put your little hand in mine.
Tell me truly that you love me,
    And—

The rest died behind her.

"He is such a nice fellow," she mused, "but there's more music in his soul than in his throat. I shall miss him today, but not so much as I shall Mr. Butler; and there is my knight of the yellow hair. Oh! I must be careful of him. He is such a direct person, there is no parrying his assault. His presence has a strange effect on me; I do not understand it; he is queer. What a pity he is not an officer, with short hair; but pshaw! I might not like him then; how absurd, I do not like him now." And thus the girlish emotions swayed her pretty head, not stopping to clarify, man fashion. They flitted about on every little wind, and alighted nowhere for more than a few seconds.

Other women joined her, and a few men, all making for the quartermaster's.

"Your mother finds herself past riding, Miss Katherine," spoke one merry matron, to whom age had been generous, and who was past it herself, did she but know it.

"Yes, mother takes that view. I am afraid I cannot sustain the reputation of the Searles outfit, as the phrase goes here. My horse is a Dobbin—papa is so absurdly careful. There is no fun in being careful."

"Oh, the Major is right. He knows the value of that little nose of yours, and doesn't want it ploughed in the dirt. Noses which point upward, just ever so little, lack the severity of those that point down, in women; that is what the men tell me, Katherine."

The girl glanced at her companion, and doubted not that the men had said that to her.

"I don't care to go through life thinking of my nose," she added.

"No, indeed; never think of your nose; think of what men think of it."

"I can go home and do that, Mrs. Gooding; out here my horse seems more to the point than my nose." At this juncture some men opened the corral gate, and the women passed in.

Seeing the wolf flattened out like an unoratorical man at a banquet, who knows he is next on the toast-list, Miss Searles exclaimed, "Poor creature! It seems such a shame."

And the others added, "Now that I see him I feel like a butcher."

"Let him go, Major; we will not have his murder on our conscience," continued a third.

"I should as soon think of killing a canary in a cage." And thus did the gentler sex fail at this stage; but when the Colonel rode out of the enclosure, they all followed.

The wolf rose to its feet with a snap as the half-breed and Ermine approached, curling their lariats. A few deft turns, and the ropes drew around the captive's throat. A man undid the chain, the horse started, and the wild beast drew after, a whizzing blur of gray hair.

There was some difficulty in passing the gate, but that was managed. The remembrance of yesterday's experience in the rawhide coils came back to the wolf. It slunk along, tail down, and with head turning in scared anxious glances. Behind followed the rearguard, waving their whips at various feeble-minded ki-yis which were emboldened by their own yelling.

"Colonel, give me a good start; this is a female wolf. I will raise my hat and drop it on the ground when it is time to let the dogs go! We may have trouble clearing away these ropes," talked Ermine, loudly.

"Sacre—mi-ka-tic-eh muck-a-muck—dees dam wolf he have already bite de hole in my rope ver near," and Wolf-Voice gave a severe jerk. To be sure, the animal was already playing havoc with his lariat by savage side-snaps which bade fair shortly to shred it.

"Watch my hat, Colonel; she may get away from us before we are ready."

Well outside of the post the Colonel halted his field and waited; all eyes bent on the two wild men, with their dangerous bait, going up the road. The nimble ponies darted about in response to the riders' swayings, while at intervals the wolf gave an imitation of a pin-wheel.

When well out, Wolf-Voice yelled, "Ah, dare go my rope!"

The wolf had cut it, and turning, fixed its eyes on Ermine, who stopped and shook his lariat carefully, rolling it in friendly circles toward the wolf. Wolf-Voice drew his gun, and for an appreciable time the situation had limitless possibilities. By the exercise of an intelligence not at all rare in wild creatures, the wolf lay down and clawed at the rope. In an instant it was free and galloping off, turning its head to study the strategy of the field.

"Wait for the people; she's going for the timber, and will get away," shouted Ermine, casting his big sombrero into the air.

The dogs held in leash never lost sight of the gray fellow, and when let go were soon whippeting along. The horses sank on their quarters and heaved themselves forward until the dusty plain groaned under their feet.

"Ki-yi-yi-yi," called the soldiers, imitating the Indians who had so often swept in front of their guns.

The wolf fled, a gray shadow borne on the wind, making for the timber in the river-bottom. It had a long start and a fair hope. If it had understood how vain the noses of greyhounds are, it might have cut its angle to cover a little; for once out of sight it might soon take itself safely off; but no wild animal can afford to angle much before the spider dogs.

The field was bunched at the start and kicked up a vast choking dust, causing many slow riders to deploy out on the sides, where they could at least see the chase and the going in front of them. Wolf-Voice and Ermine had gone to opposite sides and were lost in the rush.

Ermine's interest in the wolf departed with it. He now swung his active pony through the dirt clouds, seeking the girl, and at last found her, well in the rear as usual, and unescorted, after the usual luck she encountered when she played her charms against a wolf. She was trying to escape from the pall by edging off toward the riverbank. Well behind strode the swift war-pony, and Ermine devoured her with his eyes. The impulse to seize and bear her away to the inaccessible fastnesses of which he knew was overcome by a fear of her—a fear so great that his blood turned to water when his passion was greatest.

Time did not improve Ermine's logistics concerning this girl; he wanted her, and he did not know in the least how to get her. The tigers of his imagination bit and clawed each other in ferocious combat when he looked at her back as she rode or at her pensive photograph in the quiet of his tent. When, however, she turned the battery of her eyes on him, the fever left him in a dull, chilly lethargy—a realization of the hopelessness of his yearning; and plot and plan and assuage his fears as he might, he was always left in a mustache-biting perplexity. He could not at will make the easy reconnaissance of her fortresses which the young officers did, and this thought maddened him. It poisoned his mind and left his soul like a dead fish cast up on a riverbank.

Ermine had known the easy familiarity of the Indian squaws, but none of them had ever stirred him. The vast silence of his mountain life had rarely been broken by the presence of men, and never by women. The prophet had utterly neglected the boy's emotions in the interest of his intellect. The intense poverty of his experience left him without any understanding of the most ordinary conventions or casual affairs of white men's lives. All he knew was gathered from his observation of the rude relations of frontier soldiers on campaign. The visions of angels never exalted a fasting mediæval monk in his cell as did the advent of this white woman to Ermine, and they were quite as nebulous.

The powerful appeal which Katherine Searles made to his imagination was beyond the power of his analysis; the word Love was unknown to his vocabulary. He wanted her body, he wanted her mind, and he wanted her soul merged with his, but as he looked at her now, his mouth grew dry, like a man in mortal fear or mortal agony.

And thinking thus, he saw her horse stop dead—sink—and go heels up and over in a complete somersault. The girl fluttered through the air and struck, raising a dust which almost concealed her. A savage slap of his quirt made his pony tear the ground in his frantic rush to her aid. No one noticed the accident, and the chase swept around the bluffs and left him kneeling beside her. She showed no sign of life; the peach-blow left her cheeks an ivory white, set with pearls when the high lights showed, but there was no blood or wound which he could see.

Her mount struggled to extract his poor broken foreleg from a gopher-hole, where it was sunk to the elbow. He raised his head, with its eyes rolling, and groaned in agony.

If this had been a man, or even any other woman, Ermine would have known what to do. In his life a wounded or broken man had been a frequent experience. As he took her wrist to feel her pulse, his own hands trembled so that he gave over; he could feel nothing but the mad torrent of his own blood.

Turning his face in the direction where the hunt had gone, he yelled, "Help! Help!" but the sound never reached the thudding hunt. Putting his arm under her shoulder, he raised her up, and supporting her, he looked hopelessly around until his eye fell on the Yellowstone only a short distance away. Water had always been what the wounded wanted. He slowly gathered her in his arms, gained his feet, and made his way toward the river. A gopher-hole had planned what Ermine never could; it had brought her body to him, but it might be a useless gift unless the water gave him back her life.

He bore the limp form to the sands beside the flowing river and laid it down while he ran to fill his hat with water. He made fast work of his restoration, rubbing her wrists and sprinkling her forehead with water; but it was long before a reward came in the way of a breath and a sigh. Again he raised her in a sitting position against his knee.

"Breathe, Katherine—try again—now breathe." And he pressed her chest with his hand, aiding nature as best he knew, until she sighed again and again.

The girl was half damp in death, while like a burning mine the pent-up fire-damp exploded and reverberated through the veins of the young man. Oh, if he could but impart his vitality to her. Possibly he did, for presently her weakness permitted her to note that the sky was blue, that the treetops waved in familiar forms, that the air flooded her lungs, and that a cooling rain was falling. Again she drifted somewhere away from the earth in pleasant passage through kaleidoscopic dreams of all a girl's subconsciousness ever offers.

Her eyes spread, but soon closed in complete rest against the easy cradle. She sensed kindly caresses and warm kisses which delighted her. The long yellow hair hung about her face and kept it shadowed from the hot sun.

"Oh my! Oh my! Where am I? Is that you—How do I—" but the effort exhausted her.

"God—God—Sak-a-war-te come quick! It will be too late." He put more water on her face.

*   *   *   *   *   *

The hunt missed the wolf in the cover of the river-bottom. It doubled on the dogs, and out of sight was out of mind with the fast-running hounds.

"She gave us a run, anyhow," sang out Major Searles to Wolf-Voice.

"Yaes, d—— him; she give me a bite and two run. What good was come of eet, hey—why ain't you keel him first plass, by Gar?"

"He bore the limp form to the sands"

"Oh! You are a poor sport, Wolf-Voice."

"Am poor sport, hey? All right; nex' wolf she not tink dat, mabeso."

Laughing and talking, they trotted home, picking up belated ones who had strung behind the fastest horses.

"Where is Miss Searles, Major?" spoke one.

"That's so! Don't know; had a slow horse; by Gad, we must look this up." And the now anxious father galloped his mount. The others followed sympathetically. Rounding the bluffs, they saw Ermine's pony quietly feeding.

"Where is Ermine?" came a hail of questions, and presently they almost ran over the girl's horse, now lying on its side, breathing heavily, and no longer trying to disengage his leg from the gopher-hole.

"The horse is in a gopher-hole," said some one; "and see here— look at the dirt; he has thrown Miss Searles; here is where she struck."

"Yes, but where is she? Where is she?" ejaculated the Major, in a nervous tremor of excitement. "Where is my girl?"

Wolf-Voice had dismounted and found Ermine's trail, which he followed toward the river.

"Come!" he called. "Am show you dose girl!"

While an orderly stayed behind, to shoot the horse and get the empty saddle, the group followed hard on the half-breed.

"Done you ride on de trail, you was keep behine. Dey girl was broke his neck, an' Ermine am pack him."

Stepping briskly forward, the plainsman made quick work of empty moccasin tracks and burst through the brush. A pistol-shot rang in the rear; an orderly had shot the horse. A cry of "Help, help!" responded from the river beyond the cottonwoods, and the horses ploughed their way to the sands. The people all dismounted around the limp figure and kneeling scout. Her pale face, the hat with the water in it, and the horse in the gopher-hole made everything clear.

"Here, Swan, ride to the post for an ambulance," spoke the Major, as he too knelt and took his daughter in his arms. "Ride the horse to death and tell the ambulance to come running." Some of the women brought their ministering hands to bear and with more effect.

"What happened, Katherine?" whispered her father amid the eager silence of the gathered people.

"What did I do?" she pleaded weakly.

"How was it, Ermine?"

"Her horse put his foot in a hole; he is out there now. I saw her go down. Then I tried to save her. Will she live?"

Ermine's eager interest had not departed because of the advent of so many people. He still continued to kneel and to gaze in rapture at the creature of his hopes and fears. No one saw anything in it but the natural interest of one who had been left with so much responsibility.

"If you men will retire, we will endeavor to find her injuries," spoke one of the older ladies; so the men withdrew.

Every one asked eager questions of the scout, who walked hat in hand, and had never before shown perturbation under the trying situations in which he and the soldiers had been placed.

"I knew that wolf would get away in the timber, and I wasn't going to ride my pony for the fun of seeing it, so I was behind. Miss Searles' horse was slow, and I noticed she was being left; then she went down and I didn't know what to do"—which latter statement was true.

He had done as well under the circumstances as any man could, they all admitted. A magpie on an adjoining limb jeered at the soldiers, though he made no mention of anything further than the scout had admitted.

In due course the ambulance came bounding behind the straining mules. Mrs. Searles was on the seat with the driver, hatless, and white with fear. The young woman was placed in and taken slowly to quarters. Being the only witness, Ermine repeated his story until he grew tired of speech and wanted only silence which would enable him to think. The greatest event of his life had happened to him that morning; it had come in a curious way; it had lasted but a few moments, but it had added new fuel to his burning mind, which bade fair to consume it altogether.

Miss Searles' injuries consisted of a few bruises and a general shock from which she would soon recover, said the doctor, and the cantonment slowly regathered its composure, all except Shockley, who sat, head down, in most disordered thought, slowly punctuating events as they came to him, by beating on the floor with his scabbard.

"And she gave him her glove and she never gave me any glove— and she never gave Butler her glove that I know of; and he gave her a wolf and he was with her when this thing happened. Say, Shockley, me boy, you are too slow, you are rusty; if you saw an ancient widow woman chopping wood, you would think she was in love with the woodpile." And thus did that worthy arrive at wrong conclusions. He would not give himself the credit of being only a man, whom God in the wisdom of His creation did not intend to understand women and thus deaden a world.

The camp was in ignorance of the points of contact between Katherine Searles and the scout; it felt none of the concern which distressed Shockley.

Miss Searles had known Butler back in the States; they were much together here on the Yellowstone, and it was pretty generally admitted that insofar as she was concerned Lieutenant Butler had the biggest pair of antlers in the garrison. That young officer was a fine soldier— one of the best products of West Point, and was well connected back East, which was no small thing in an affair of this nature. Also his fellows easily calculated that he must have more than his pay. Shockley, however, continued to study the strategy of the scout Ermine, and he saw much to fear.

CHAPTER SEVENTEEN

A PROPOSAL

"OH! I SAY, CAPTAIN LEWIS, I AM ALL ready to start. I have Ramon, a cook, and Wolf-Voice, together with pack-animals, but I can't get your man Ermine to say when he will go."

"That's odd, Harding; I don't know of anything to detain him. But go slow; he's like all these wild men up here; when they will they will, and when they won't, they'll lay down on you. I'll go round and scout him up. What is the matter so far as you can determine?"

"I can't determine. He says he will go, but will not name any exact time; tells me to push on and that he will catch up. That is a curious proposition. He is willing to take my money—"

"Oh! Whoa up, Mr. Harding! That fellow doesn't care anything about your money—make no mistake about that. Money means no more to him than to a blue jay. He wanted to go back to his own country and was willing, incidentally, to take you. I'll see; you wait here awhile"; saying which, Captain Lewis went in search of his man, whom he found whittling a stick pensively.

"Hello, my boy, you don't seem to be very busy. Suppose your heart is out in the hills chasing the elk and bear."

"No, Captain; I don't care much about the hills."

"Or the Crow squaws?"

"D—— the Crow squaws!" And Ermine emphasized this by cutting his stick through the middle.

"Want to stay here?"

"Yes, I am getting so I like this camp; like the soldiers—like the wagons—kind of like the whole outfit."

"Like to chase wolves?" interrupted the officer.

Ermine slowly turned up his head and settled his fathomless blue eyes on Lewis, but he said nothing.

"Well, Mr. Harding is all set. You said you would go with him; a soldier must keep his word."

"I will go with him."

"When?"

Again Ermine shaved some delicate slivers off the stick; suddenly he threw it away, shut up his knife, and arose. "If Mr. Harding will pull out now, Wolf-Voice will show him the way. I shall know where the Indian takes him, and in four days I will walk into his camp. The pack-ponies travel slowly, I do not care to punch packhorses; that will do for Ramon and the cook."

"Does that go?"

"I have said it. Did I ever lie, Captain Lewis?"

"All right. Mr. Harding will go now. I will attend to that." With this Lewis left him, and in two hours the little cavalcade trotted westward, out into the hot, sunlit plains, carrying faith in Ermine's word. The scout, leaning on a log stable, saw them go.

Three days took their slow departure, and on the morrow Ermine would have to make good his word to follow the Englishmen. He would have liked to stay even if his body suffered slow fire, but excuses would not avail for his honor. A soldier's honor was something made much of in these parts; it pegged higher than the affairs of the flesh.

He had not been able to see Miss Searles, and he wondered what she would feel, or think, or say. He was a thief when he remembered the stolen kisses, and he dared not go to the Searleses' home to inquire after her. All this diffidence the public put down to apathy; he had done his duty, so why further concern himself?

After supper he strolled along the officers' row, desperately forlorn, but hoping and yearning, barely nodding his head to passersby.

Major Searles approached him with the nervous stride habitual to a soldier, and held out his hand, saying bluffly: "Of course, I can't thank you enough for your attention to my daughter, Ermine. But for your fortunate presence there at the time of the accident, things might have been bad; how bad I fear to contemplate. Come to my quarters, my boy, and allow my daughter to thank you. She is quite recovered. She is sitting out-of-doors. She hasn't been abroad much. Such a fall would have killed an older woman."

Together they made their way to the house, and Ermine passed under the *ramada* with his hat off. Mrs. Searles shook his hand and said many motherly things due on such occasions.

"Please forgive me if I do not rise; it is the doctor's orders, you know." And Miss Searles extended her hand, which the scout reverently took. To have seen him one would have fancied that, after all, manners must have been made before men; which idea is, of course, absurd.

In response to their inquiries, he retold the story of the accident and of his ministrations and perplexities. He did not embellish, but left out very important details, wondering the while if they were dead to all but his memory.

"She should not ride so poor a horse," ventured Ermine.

"She should not have been left unattended." And this severity was directed at Major Searles by his wife, to which he feebly pleaded vain extenuations, without hope of their acceptance.

"No, no, my dear; you were always a careless person; one is never safe to place dependence on you in minor matters. I declare, all men are alike—leastwise soldiers are. A blanket and a haversack, and the world may wag at will, so far as they concern themselves." Rising, she adjusted her hat, saying: "I must run down to Mrs. Taylor's for a minute. Her baby is very ill, and she has sent for me. You will stay here, Major," and she swept out.

"When do you depart for your hunting with Mr. Harding, Ermine?" asked Searles.

"I must go soon. He left camp three days ago, and I have promised to follow."

"I should think you would be delighted to hunt. I know I should if I were a man," cheerfully remarked the young woman.

"I have always hunted, Miss Searles. I think I should like to do something else."

"What, pray?"

"Oh, I don't know, something with a white shirt in it."

"Isn't that foolish? There is no more fun in a white shirt than there is in a buckskin one, and there is no fun in either when it rains, I am told."

A passing officer appealed to the Major to come out; he was needed, together with other requests to follow, with reasons why haste was important.

"All right, I will be back in a moment, daughter." And the officer took himself off in complete disobedience of his wife's orders.

"Don't be gone long, father; there is no one here but Mary and the striker. You know I cannot depend on them."

"You keep the wolves off, Ermine; I won't be gone a minute." And Ermine found himself alone again with Katherine.

This time she was not pale unto death, but warm and tingling. Her lover's hands and feet took better care of themselves on a horse than in a chair, but the gloom under the porch at least stayed some of the embarrassment which her eyes occasioned him. Indeed, it is well known that lovers prefer night attacks, and despite the law and the prophets, they manage better without an audience.

She gained a particularly entrancing attitude in her chair by a pussy-cat wiggle which let the point of her very small foot out of concealing draperies. One hand hung limply toward Ermine over the arm of the chair, and it seemed to scream out to him to take hold of it.

"And when do you go, Mr. Ermine?"

This seemed safe, and along the lines of his self-interest.

"I go tomorrow; I have given my word."

"Very naturally there can be nothing to delay you here," she continued; "the fighting is over, I hear."

"There is something in the world beside fighting."

"Yes?" she evaded.

"Yes, you detain me."

"I!" and the little foot went back to its nest; the extended hand rose in protest. "I detain you! My dear Mr. Ermine, I do not understand how I detain you; really, I am quite recovered from my fall."

"You may have got well, Miss Searles, but I am not. Do you remember?"

"Remember—remember—do I remember? What should I remember? I am told you were very good to me, but I was laboring under such a shock at the time that you cannot expect much of my memory."

"I was but little better off."

"And were you injured also?"

"Yes, so bad that I shall never get well unless you come to my rescue."

"I come to your rescue! What can I do?" Her sword waved in tierce and seconde.

"Be my wife; come, girl, be my wife."

He had beaten down her guard; the whole mass was in the fire. The dam had broken; he led his forlorn hope into the breach. "Come, Katherine, say you will marry me; say it and save me."

"Oh," she almost screamed, "I can't do that; why, my mother would never consent to it," she appealed in bewilderment.

He had risen and taken a step forward. "What has your mother to say? Say you will be my wife, Katherine."

"Careful, careful, Mr. Ermine; restrain yourself, or I shall call a servant. No, no, I cannot marry you. Why, what should we do if I did? We should have to live in the mule corral."

"No, come to the mountains with me. I will make you a good camp."

She almost laughed aloud at this. "But I should make a poor squaw. I fear you would have many quarrels with your dinner. Besides, my father would not let me marry you. I like you, and you have been very good to me, but I had no idea we had gotten so far as this. Don't you think you Western men cover the ground a little too fast?"

Ermine drew back. "Why did you kiss me?"

"I didn't," she snapped. Her manner grew cold and strange to him. He had never seen this mood before. It chilled him not a little, and he sat down again in the chair. His assault had been repulsed. They were now looking straight into each other's eyes. Fear had departed from Ermine's and all graciousness from hers. Divested of their seductive flashes, he saw the eyes of his photograph, and slowly reaching into the bosom of his shirt, drew out the buckskin bag and undid it. Turning to the straining light, he gazed a moment, and then said, "It is you!"

"I! What is I?"

"Yes! It is you!" and he handed the much-soiled photograph labelled "Bogardus" to her.

She regarded it. "Why, how on earth did you come by this, Mr. John Ermine?"

"Sak-a-war-te sent it to me in the night, and he made it talk to me and he made me swear that I would seek the woman until I found her. Then she would be my wife. I have found you—I do not know—my head is burning—"

She scanned the photograph, and said in an undertone: "Taken last year in New York, and for him; yet you have it away out here in the middle of this enormous desert. He surely would not give it away to you. I do not understand." And she questioned him sharply as she returned the card.

"Who is this Sak-a-war-te?"

"He is God," said the scout.

"Oh!" she started up. The little miss had never heard God connected with affairs of this sort. An active fear of the fire which burned this extraordinary man's head began to oppress her.

"It is very strange. What has your god got to do with me—with my—oh, you are joking, Mr. Ermine," she again appealed, a shadow of her old smile appearing.

"No, no; I am not joking. I have found you. I must believe what the spirits say to me when they take my mind from me and give it to you," returned the excited man.

"But really—I did not mean to take your mind. I haven't it anywhere about me. You have dreamed all this."

"Yes; it may be only a dream, Miss Searles, but make it come true; please make it all come true. I should like to live such a dream."

"Oh, my good man, I cannot make the dreams of casual people come true, not such serious dreams as yours."

"You say you would have to live in the corral with mules. Is that because I have so little money?"

"No, it is not money. I do not know how much you have."

"I have often taken enough gold out of the ground in a few days to last me a year."

"Yes, yes, but that is not the only thing necessary."

"What is necessary, then? Tell me what you want."

"There would have to be a great deal of love, you know. That is why any one marries. I have been flattered by the attentions of many cavaliers like yourself, Mr. Ermine, but I could not marry any one of them unless I loved him."

"And then you do not love me," this in a low, far-away voice, lopping each word off as though with an axe.

"No, I do not. I have given you no reason to think I did. I like you, and I am sorry for you, now that I know in what way you regard me. Sit down again and let me tell you." She crouched herself on the edge of her chair, and he sat in his, revolving his big hat in both hands between his knees. He was composed, and she vaguely felt that she owed him a return for his generous acts of the past. She had the light touch of mature civilization and did not desire her darts to be deadly. Now that one had laid this simple nature low, she felt a womanly impulse to nurse the wound.

"Some terrible mistake has been made. Believe me, I am truly sorry that our relationship has not been rightly understood." Here she paused a moment to take a long breath and observe the effect of her words on the one who had so easily lost his head. "No, I simply admired you, Mr. Ermine, as I do many of the brave men about here. I was not thinking of marrying any one. As for living in the mule corral, I was only joking about that. There might be worse places. I should dearly love a gold mine, but don't you understand there would have to be something else—I should have to give you something before we thought of marrying."

"I see it; it all comes to me now," he labored. "You would have to give me something, and you won't give me yourself. Then give me back my mind—give me the peace which I always had until I saw you. Can you do that, Miss Searles? Can you make John Ermine what he was before the steamboat came here, and let him mount his pony and go away?"

It was all so strange, this quiet appeal, that she passed her hand across her forehead in despair.

"If you will not make my dreams come true; if you will not say the things which the photograph does; if you will not do what God intends—then I must take my body away from here and leave my shadow, my mind, and my heart to be kicked about among the wagons and the dogs. And I know now that you will soon forget me. Then I will be John Ermine, riding among the hills, empty as an old buffalo carcass, moving without life, giving no thought to the sunshine, not feeling the wind nor caring how the birds fly or the animals run. If you will not marry me—"

"Stop, please stop. I cannot stand this sort of thing, my dear Mr. Ermine. There are other young women besides myself. Go about the world, back in the States; you will find whole oceans of them, and without flattery, I feel you will soon find your mind again."

"You have my mind. You have all the mind I ever had." And his voice dropped until she could distinguish only wild gutturals. He was talking to himself in the Indian language.

Springing up quickly, she flew into the house, out through it to the rear steps, where she fell upon the neck of Mary, the cook, to the utter consternation of a soldier, who, to all appearances, was there with a similar ambition so to do. This latter worthy flung himself out into the darkness. The cook held Katherine, expecting the entire Sioux tribe to come pouring through the front door on the instant, and at this belated interval Mrs. Searles entered her own porch.

"Why, Mr. Ermine, where is Katherine, and where is the Major? Why, you are all alone!" And she came up standing.

"Yes, I am all alone," said the scout, quietly, rising from the chair and putting on his sombrero. Before she could comprehend, he was gone.

CHAPTER EIGHTEEN

MAN TO MAN

T HE MAJOR SAUNTERED IN SHORTLY AND FOUND Mrs. Searles standing over Katherine's chair, trying to dry her tears and gather the reasons for her grief. Mary's Indians not having appeared, she stood in the doorway, with her apron raised to a sort of feminine "charge bayonets."

"What in the devil is the circus?" demanded the father.

"It's nothing, father; I am nervous, that is all."

"Now, Major Searles, I want you to sit down and keep quiet. You will drive me frantic. Why did you run away when I clearly told you to stay here?" Her tones were dry with formality.

Against all manner of people and happenings the Major joyfully pitted his force and cunning. His only thought in a great crisis was his six-shooter; but he always hesitated before anything which concerned Mrs. Searles and a military order. These impelled obedience from the very nature of things. "But what has happened? What must I do?"

"You must sit down," said his wife; and he sat down. Affairs of this kind could be cleared only by women; he was conscious that he could not hurry matters.

"Now what has happened, Katherine? Will you tell me? Who did it?" pleaded the mother.

"Why, it is nothing, only that horrible scout wanted to marry me. Did you ever hear anything so ridiculous?" said the girl, sitting up and made defiant by the idea.

"Did he do anything?" and the Major again forgot his orders and rose truculently.

"Benjamin!" said Mrs. Searles, with asperity; and he again subsided. Like most soldiers and sailors, he was imperfectly domesticated.

"He wanted to marry you?" she continued with questioning insistence.

"Yes, he said I must marry him; that God wanted me to, and he also said he had lost his mind—"

"Well, I think he has," observed the mother, catching this idea, which was at least tangible to her. "Is that all, Katherine?"

"Is that all, mother? Why, isn't that enough?"

"I mean, he simply asked you to marry him—properly—he wasn't insulting—insistent beyond—"

"No, he did nothing else, though he went about it in a most alarming way."

"You said, No!"

"I most emphatically did, mother."

"What then?"

"Then he began mumbling Indian and scared me nearly to death. I ran to Mary."

"Dade an' she did, mum; an' I'm afther loosin' my sinses thinkin' thim rid-divils what do be ploughin' the land down be the river was devastating the cantonmint for to pass the time. An' ets only some bye afther wantin' to marry her—the swate thing."

Mrs. Searles interposed, "Mary!" and the domestic retired to the sable silences of the rear steps, to split a joke with one Private O'Shane, should he venture to return.

"The social savagery of this place is depressing. To think of my daughter living in a log-cabin, cooking bear meat for a long-haired wild man. In the future, Benjamin Searles, I trust you will not feel called upon to introduce your fantastic acquaintances to this house. You can sit on the corral fence to entertain them. That is where they belong. I suppose next, an out-and-out Indian will want to be my son-in-law."

"I certainly will see that the man does not again obtrude himself. I do not understand his nerve in this matter. Lewis thinks the boy's ridgepole is crooked; but he is harmless and has done many good and gallant deeds. As for his proposing, I simply think he doesn't know any better. For my part, I think it is about time that the engagement to Mr. Butler is announced; it will put an end to this foolishness all round," added the father. "I am going out to see Lewis about this fellow now."

"Ben Searles, I hope you are not going to do anything rash," pleaded the mother.

"Of course not, my dear; the situation doesn't call for any temperature beyond blood-heat. I only want to put a cooling lotion on the base of that scout's brain. He must stop this dreaming habit."

Having found Lewis at his quarters and seated himself, the Major began, "Now, Captain, what do you think of this Ermine of yours—is he crazy?"

"Is he crazy? Why, what has he done now?"

"Well, by Gad, he came to my house this evening, and when I stepped out for a minute he proposed marriage to my daughter—wanted her to marry him! Now, how's that strike you? Is it just gall, or does he need a physician?"

"Well, I will be d——d; proposed marriage, hey! Looks like he ought to have an opiate," concluded Lewis. "You know, now that I think of it, I have a little mistrusted him before. He has shown signs of liking your daughter, but I never regarded the matter seriously—didn't ever credit him with being an entire fool. The boy's queer, Searles—mighty queer, but he never did anything wrong; in fact, he is a pretty good boy—a heap different from most of these double-belted, sagebush terrors. Then, of course, he was born and raised in the wilderness, and there is a whole lot of things he don't savvy. Probably he has lost his head over your daughter and he can't see why he hasn't a chance. I will send for him, and we will make a big talk, and I'll send him away to Harding." Turning, the Captain yelled, "Orderly! Jones! Oh, Jones!"

"Yes, sir," responded Jones, as he appeared in the doorway.

"Go find the scout Ermine, if you can, and tell him to report to me immediately. If you don't find him in half an hour, let it go until tomorrow—understand?

"As I was saying, you see, Major, if this thing wasn't vinegar, it would be sugar. When I think of him proposing—say, I have to laugh. There is one thing about him which kept me guessing: it is the Indian reserve of the fellow. He goes round here like a blue-moon, and if you should hit him over the head with an axe, I don't think he would bat an eye. He never complains, he never questions, and when you are right up against it, as we were a half-dozen times last winter, he is Johnny-on-the-spot. So you see, if he fell in love, no one would hear the splash. Now that he is in love, we want to tighten the curb chain; he might—well, he might take it into his head to do something, and that something might be just what we would never think of."

Thus the two speculated until the sandpaper grating of Ermine's moccasins on the porch warned them, and looking up they beheld the scout, standing with his rifle in the hollow of his left arm. This was unusual and produced several seconds of very bad silence. Captain Lewis held up his hand in mockery of the "peace sign," and said: "I see you're fixed for war, Ermine. Sit down over there. I want to talk to you."

The scout removed his hat and sat down, but with the ominous rifle in place. He had been told by the orderly whom he was to encounter; and it had come over him that wanting to marry Katherine Searles might be some crime against the white man's law. He had seen very natural actions of men punished under those laws during his sojourn in camp.

"Ermine, I understand that during the temporary absence of her father this evening, you asked Miss Searles to marry you."

"I did, sir."

"Very well. Don't you think you took an unfair advantage of her father's absence?"

"I don't know, sir. A man doesn't speak to a woman before other men," replied Ermine, dubiously.

The Captain emitted a slight cough, for the blow had staggered him a little. He knew the law of convention, and he knew the customs of men; but they did not separate readily in his mind.

"In any event, Ermine, the young lady had given you no encouragement which would warrant you in going to the length of proposing marriage to her."

This was an assertion which Ermine did not care to discuss. His views would not coincide, and so he fumbled his hat and made no reply.

"I may state that you are not warranted in aspiring to the hand of Miss Searles for many reasons; further, that she distinctly doesn't want attention of any kind from you. To this I will add, her father and mother forbid you all association in the future—do you understand?"

This, also, failed to break the scout's silence.

"And," interpolated the father, "I may add that my daughter is already engaged to be married to Lieutenant Butler, which will end the matter."

If the evening's occurrences had set the nerves of the Searles family on edge, it had torn the scout's into shreds; but he managed his stoicism.

"Now, my boy," continued Captain Lewis, with a sense of benevolence, "we do not mean to be hard on you. We all, including Miss Searles, feel a great pity for you in this matter."

"Pity—pity—what is pity?" saying which the boy's eyes took on an unnatural glow and he rose to his feet. Lewis quickly added, "I mean that we feel for you."

"I know what you feel for me, Captain Lewis, and Major Searles," and it was evident that Ermine was aroused. "You feel that I am an uneducated man, without money, and that I do not wear a white shirt; that I tuck my pants in my leggings and that I sleep among the Indians. I know you think I am a dog. I know Miss Searles thinks I belong in the corral with the mules; but, by G——, you did not think I was a dog when the Sioux had your wagon-train surrounded and your soldiers buffaloed; you did not think I was a dog when I stood beside the Colonel, and neither did Sitting Bull. You did not think I was a dog when I kept you all from freezing to death last winter; but here among the huts and the women I am a dog. I tell you now that I do not understand such men as you are. You have two hearts: one is red and the other is blue; and you feel with the one that best suits you at the time. Your blue heart pities me. Me, a warrior and a soldier! Do you give pity with your coffee and sow-belly? Is that what you feed a soldier on? Hum-m—G——!" And the scout slapped his hat on his head.

"Steady, steady, my boy; don't you go up in the air on us," said Lewis, persuasively. "I did not mean to offend you, and we want to be friends; but you keep your feet on the ground and don't go raring and pitching, or we may forget you."

"Yes; that is it—forget me; you may forget me. What's more, you can do it now. I am going far away, so that your eyes will not remind you."

"You are going to make your word good to Mr. Harding, are you not?" asked the chief of scouts.

"What good is a dog's word?" came the bitter reply.

The Major said little, but remained steadily studying the face of the scout; rising, he approached him with extended hand. "If you are going away, let us part friends, at least. Here is my hand, and I shall not forget you; I shall not forget your services to me or mine, and I do not think you are a dog. When you calm down you may find that you have been unjust to Captain Lewis and myself."

The scout took the Major's hand mechanically, and also that of Lewis, which the latter offered in turn, saying:

"In the morning I will see that you get your pay, and if you conclude to return, I will find you employment."

"Thank you, sir; I care nothing for the pay. I did not come here for money; I came here to help you fight the Sioux, and to be a man among white men." And once more the young man relapsed into the quiet of his ordinary discourse.

"You certainly have shown yourself a man among men; no one has ever questioned that," said the Major.

"Then why is it wrong for a man among men to want your daughter to be his wife?"

"It is not wrong, but you have gone about the matter wrong. I have tried to make it plain that her hand is promised to Mr. Butler."

As this was said, two horses trotted up to Captain Lewis' quarters. A man dismounted, gave his horse to the other, and Butler himself strode heavily into the room. He was quite gray with dust, with a soiled handkerchief about his neck, unshaven, booted, and armed.

"Hello, Major! Hello, Lewis! I'm just in with my troop, and if you will pardon me, I will have a word with Mr. Ermine here." His manner was strained, and knowing the situation as they all did, the two older officers were alarmed.

"Hold up there, Butler; never mind your word tonight; wait until morning."

Butler paid no attention, but addressed the scout with icy directness. "May I ask, Mr. Ermine, if you have in your possession a photograph of Miss Searles?"

"I have."

"Have you it about your person at present?"

"I have, sir."

"Then, Mr. Ermine, I have the word of Miss Searles for it, that the photograph in question was one she had taken, of which there is only one copy in the world; and which was given to me, and lost by myself, somewhere on the road between here and Fort Ellis. It must be my property. If you will let me see it, I can soon identify it. In which case I demand that you hand it over to me."

"Mr. Butler, you will only get that photograph from off my dead body. You have Miss Searles; is not that enough?"

"I will then take it by force from you!" A tremendous bang roared around the room, and the little group was lost in smoke.

Butler turned half round, his six-shooter going against the far wall with a crash. He continued to revolve until caught in the Major's arms. Lewis sprang to his desk, where his pistol lay, and as he turned, the smoke lifted, revealing Butler lying against the Major's chest, wildly waving his left arm and muttering savagely between short breaths. Ermine was gone.

"Fire on that man!" yelled Lewis to the orderly outside, taking one shot himself at the fleeing figure of the scout.

The soldier jerked his carbine and thrashed about the breech-block with a cartridge. "I can't see him, Captain!" he shouted.

"Fire at him, anyway! Fire, I tell you!" And the man discharged his rifle in the direction in which Ermine's figure had disappeared.

Simultaneously with the shots, the garrison bugles were drawling "Taps," but they left off with an expiring pop. The lights did not go

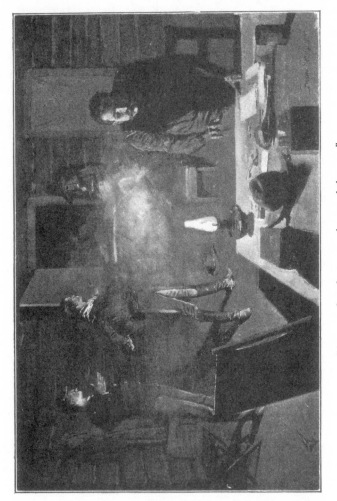

"A tremendous bang roared around the room"

out in quarters, and the guard turned out with much noise of shoe leather and rattle of guns. This body soon arrived, and Lewis spoke from the porch of his quarters.

"The scout, Ermine, has just shot Lieutenant Butler in the arm! He ran that way! Chase him! Go quickly, or he will get away. Shoot instantly if he resists; and he will, I think."

The guard shuffled off in the darkness and beat up the camp to no purpose. The soldiers stood about, speculating in low voices and gradually quieting as the word passed about on the uneasy wings of gossip that Ermine had shot Butler in the arm, wounding him badly, and that the scout had gone into the earth or up in the air, for divil the hide nor hair of him could the guard find.

When the orderly had come for Ermine and told him who wanted to see him, the scout scented trouble ahead. According to the immemorial practices of the desert at such times, he had saddled his pony, tying him in the darkest and most unlikely place he could find, which was between two six-mule wagons outside the corral. He armed himself and obeyed the summons, but he intended never to let a hand be placed on his shoulder; and he chose death rather than the military court which sat so gravely around the long table at headquarters. He fully expected to depart for the mountains on the morrow, but his hand was forced. The quick episode of Butler, ending in the shot and his flight, had precipitated matters. Shortly he found himself seated on his horse between the wagons, while the denizens of the cantonments swarmed around. A group searched the corral with lanterns, and he heard one soldier tell another what had happened, with the additional information that Butler was not seriously injured. Armed men passed close to him, and he knew that discovery meant probable death, because he would not hold up his hands. Despite the deadly danger which encompassed him, he found time for disappointment in the news that Butler was only wounded. Even now he would go to his enemy and make more sure, but that enemy was in the hospital surrounded by many friends. She, too, was probably there, weeping and hating the responsible one—a fugitive criminal driven into the night. The silken robes of self-respect had been torn from Ermine, and he stood naked, without the law, unloved by women, and with the hand of all men turned against him. The brotherhood of the white kind, which had promised him so much, had ended by stealing the heart and mind of the poor mountain boy, and now it wanted his body to work its cold will on; but it could have that only dead. This he knew as he loosed five cartridges, putting them between his teeth and clutching his loaded rifle. Would the search never cease? The lanterns glided hither and yon; every garrison cur ran yelping; the dull shuffling of feet was coming directly to the wagons which stood apart from other objects, and a dog ran under the wagon. With their eyes on the ground, an officer and two men towered above the light of a lantern. They were coming directly to the wagons. He kicked the pony and galloped softly out. Instantly the men began calling, "Halt! Halt! G—— d—— you, halt!" but the ghostly pony only answered feebly the lantern light. "Bang! Bang! Bang!" came the shots, which "zee-weeped" about his ears. He doubled quickly in the dark and trotted to the edge of the camp, which buzzed loudly behind him. He knew he must pass the sentries, but he took the chance. His apprehensions were quickly answered. "Halt!" the man was very near, but it was very dark. "Bang!" it missed, and he was away. He stopped shortly, dismounted, and ran his hand completely over the body of the pony; it was dry. "Good!" For a half-hour he walked over the herd-grounds, crossing, circling, and stopping; then back as near to the post as he dared. At last he turned and rode away. He was thoroughly familiar with the vicinity of the camp, and had no trouble so long as the post lights guided him.

The mountain boy had brought little to the soldier camp but the qualities of mind which distinguished his remote ancestors of the north of Europe, who came out of the dark forests clad in skins, and bearing the first and final law of man, a naked sword on a knotted arm. An interval of many centuries intervened between him and his fellows; all the race had evolved, all the laws which they had made for the government of society, all the subtle customs which experience had decreed should circumscribe associates, were to him but the hermit's gossip in idle hours at the cabin. The bar sinister was on his shield; his credentials were the advice of an unreal person to fight in common with the whites. He came clad in skins on a naked horse, and could barely understand English when it was in the last adulteration; and still he had made his way without stumbling until the fatal evening. Now he was fleeing for life because he had done two of the most natural things which a man can do.

"Good-by, good-by, white men, and good-by, white woman; the frost is in your hearts, and your blood runs like the melting snow from the hills. When you smile, you only skin your fangs; and when you laugh, your eyes do not laugh with you. You say good words which mean nothing. You stroke a man's back as a boy does a dog's, and kick him later as a boy does. You, woman, you who pick men's hearts and eat them as a squaw does wild plums, I want no more of you. You, Butler, I wish were out here in the dark with me; one of us would never see the sun rise. You would force me!" and the scout vented himself in a hollow laugh which was chill with murder.

The lights were lost behind the rise of the land, and the pony trotted along. No horse or man not raised on the buffalo range could travel in that darkness; but both of them made steady progress.

"Those Indians will have to crawl on their knees a whole day to pick up my pony tracks on the hard ground. The Crows will never try to follow me; the Shoshone may when the white men offer a reward. That fool of a boy may see his chance to even up the insult which I gave before the woman. He can shake her hand now for all I would do. I will ride for two hours before the sun comes, and then let the pony feed."

Patting his horse's neck, he added: "And then, my boy, we will blind our trail in some creek. I will rub the medicine on your heels, you shall gallop until dark, and no horse in that camp will get near enough to spoil my sleep."

Keeping along the river flats, floundering occasionally and dismounting to lead through the dry washes, he kept steadily on, impelled by the fear that the Indian scouts and cavalry might not stop for his trail, but deploy out at daybreak, and ride fast to the west, in the hopes that he had not yet made a long start in the darkness. There was only the danger that his horse might lame himself in the night; but then he could go back in the hills and make a skulk on foot. Even to be brought to bay had no great terror; Ermine held his life lightly in the hollow of his hand.

He mused as he rode: "They took my hair out of the braids and let it flow in the wind; then they said I was a white man. I may be one; but I wish now I had forgotten my color and I would not be so empty-handed this night. If I had followed my Indian heart, I could have stolen that girl out from under the noses of those soldiers, and I may do it yet. When she was riding, I could have taken her away from the hunting-party, rawhided her on to her horse, and left no more sign than a bird behind us; but when she looked at me, my blood turned to water. O Sak-a-war-te, why did you not take the snake's gaze out of her eyes, and not let poor Ermine sit like a gopher to be swallowed? God, God, have you deserted me?"

CHAPTER NINETEEN

FLIGHT

ERMINE UNDERSTOOD THE "talking wire," the telegraph had been made plain to him—and he knew the soldiers were stretching one into the west. He sheered away from the white man's medicine, going up a creek where only the silent waters swirling about his horse's legs could know the story of his ride, which secret they would carry to the eternal sea.

The gallant pony's blood was rich from the grain-sacks; he had carried a rider in the strain of many war-trails, and his heart had not yet failed. In the prime of life, he was now asked to do the long, quick distance that should lose the white man; those mighty people who bought the help of mercenary men; whose inexhaustible food came in the everlasting wagons; and who spoke to each other twenty sleeps apart. His rider had violated their laws, and they would have him. Only the pony could save.

Having walked the bed of the creek as far as he deemed necessary, Ermine backed his pony out of the stream into some low bushes, where he turned him about and rode away. All day over the yellow plains and through the defiles of the hills loped the fugitive. Once having seen buffalo coming in his direction, he travelled for miles along a buffalo path which he judged they would follow. If by fortune they did, he knew it would make the scouts who came after rub their eyes and smoke many pipes in embarrassment. Not entirely satisfied with his precautions—for he thought the Indians would cast ahead when checked—he continued to urge the pony steadily forward. The long miles which lay before his pursuers would make their hearts weak and their ponies' forelegs wobble.

He reflected that since he was indeed going to join Mr. Harding's party at the secret place in Gap-full-of-arrow-holes, why would not Lewis' scouts follow the easy trail made by their ponies and trust to finding him with them; and again, would the Englishman want his company under his altered status? This he answered by saying that no horse in the cantonment could eat up the ground with his war-pony; and as for the Englishman, he could not know of the late tragedy unless the accused chose to tell him. What of his word? Why was he keeping it? With a quick bullet from his rifle had gone his honor, along with other things more material. Still, the Gap lay in his way, so he could stop without inconvenience, at least long enough for a cup of coffee and some tobacco. The suddenness of his depar-ture had left him no time to gather the most simple necessities, and he was living by his gun. Only once did he see Indians far away in the shimmer of the plains. He had dropped into the dry washes and sneaked away. They might be Crows, but the arrows of doubt made sad surgery in his poor brain; the spell of the white man's vengeance was over him. Their arms were long, their purses heavy; they could turn the world against him. From their strong log-towns they would conjure his undoing by the devious methods which his experience with them had taught him to dread. The strain of his thoughts made his head ache as he cast up the events which had forced him to this wolfing through the lonely desert. He had wanted to marry a pretty girl whose eyes had challenged him to come on, and when he had ventured them, like a mountain storm the whole cantonment rattled about his head and shot its bolts to kill. As the girl had fled his pres-ence at the mere extension of his hand, in swift response to her emotions the whole combination of white humanity was hard on the heels of his flying pony.

*   *   *   *   *   *

From the summit of the red cliffs Ermine looked down into the secret valley of his quest, and sitting there beside a huge boulder he studied the rendezvous. There were Ramon's pack-ponies—he remembered them all. There curled the smoke from the tangle of brushwood in the bottom, and finally Wolf-Voice and Ramon came out to gather in the horses for the night. He rode down toward them. Their quick ears caught the sound of the rattle of the stones loosened by his mount, and they stopped. He waved his hat, and they recognized him. He came up and dismounted from his drooping horse, stiff-hided with lather and dust, hollow-flanked, and with his belly drawn up as tight as the head of a tom-tom.

"Are you alone in the camp? Has no one been here?"

"No; what for waas any one been here?" asked and answered the half-breed. "De King George Man, she waas set by dose fire an' waas ask me 'bout once a minit when waas Ermine come."

The men drove the horses in while Ermine made his way through the brush to the campfire.

"Aha! Glad to see you, Mr. Ermine. Gad! But you must have put your horse through. He is barely holding together in the middle. Picket him out, and we will soon have some coffee going."

Ermine did as directed and was soon squatting before the fire with his cup and plate. To the hail of questions he made brief response, which Harding attributed to fatigue and the inclination of these half-wild men not to mix discourse with the more serious matter of eating.

"How did you leave every one at the camp?"

Ermine borrowed a pipe and interspersed his answers with puffs.

"Left them in the night—and they were all sitting up to see me off. My pony is weak, Mr. Harding. Will you give me a fresh one in the morning? We ought to start before daylight and make a long day of it."

"My dear man, before daylight? Are we in such haste? It seems that we have time enough before us."

"This is a bad country here. Indians of all tribes are coming and going. We are better off back in the range. In two or three sleeps we will be where we can lie on the robe, but not here"; saying which, Ermine rolled up in his saddle blanket, and perforce the others did likewise, in view of the short hours in store.

The last rasping, straining pack-rope had been laid while yet the ghostly light played softly with the obscurity of the morning. The ponies were forced forward, crashing through the bushes, floundering in the creek, cheered on by hoarse oaths, all strange to the ear of Harding. The sedate progression of other days was changed to a fox-trot—riding-whips and trail-ropes slapping about the close-hugged tails of the horses.

Harding congratulated himself on the unexpected energy of his guide; it would produce results later when wanted in the hunting. The ponies strung out ahead to escape the persecution of the lash, but Wolf-Voice saw something new in it all, and as he rode, his fierce little eyes gleamed steadily on Ermine. The half-breed knew the value of time when he was pushing the horses of the enemy away from their lodges, but these horses had no other masters. He turned his pony alongside of Ermine's.

"Say, John, what for you waas keep look behin'? Who you 'fraid follar dese pony? Ain't dose Canada-man pay for dese pony—sacre, what you was do back de camp dare? De Sioux, she broke hout?" And the half-breed's mischievous eye settled well on his confrère.

"Well, I did that back there which will make the high hills safer for me than any other place. Don't say anything to Mr. Harding until I feel safe. I want to think."

"You waas shoot some one, mabeso?"

"Yes—that—— —— Butler. He said he would force me to give up the paper we found in the moonlight on the soldier trail down the Yellowstone a year ago. He pulled his pistol, and I shot him."

"You kiell heem—hey?"

"No, caught him in the arm, but it will not kill him. I may go back and do that—when the soldiers forget a little."

"Den you waas run away—hey?"

"Yes; I made the grass smoke from Tongue River to here. I don't think they can follow me, but they may follow this party. That's why I look behind, Wolf-Voice, and that's why I want you to look behind."

"What for you waas come to de King George Man, anyhow?"

"I wanted coffee and tobacco and a fresh pony and more cartridges, and it will be many moons before John Ermine will dare look in a trader's store. If the white men come, I will soon leave you; and if I do, you must stay and guide Mr. Harding. He is a good man and does what is right by us."

"Ah!" hissed the half-breed, "old Broken-Shoe and White-Robe, she ain' let dose Engun follar you. You spose dey let dose Crow tak de ack-kisr-attah to Crooked-Bear's boy? Humph, dey 'fraid of hees medecin'."

"Well, they will pile the blankets as high as a horse's back, and say to the Shoshone, 'Go get the yellow-hair, and these are your blankets.' What then?"

"Ugh! Ugh! A-nah," grunted the half-breed; "de—— —— Shoshone, we will leek de pony—come—come!"

The energy of the march, the whacking ropes, and scampering horses passed from satisfaction to downright distress in Mr. Harding's mind. He pleaded for more deliberation, but it went unheeded. The sun had gone behind the hard blue of the main range before they camped, and the good nature of the Englishman departed with it.

"Why is it necessary to break our cattle down by this tremendous scampering? It does not appeal to my sense of the situation."

"Wael, meester, wan more sun we waas en de hiell—den we have long smoke; all you waas do waas sit down smoke your pipe—get up—kiell dose grizzly bear—den sit down some more."

But this observation of the half-breed's was offset by Ramon, who was cleaning a frying pan with a piece of bread, and screwing his eyes into those of Wolf-Voice. The matter was not clear to him. "What good can come of running the legs off the ponies? Why can't we sit down here and smoke?"

"You waas trader—you waas spend all de morning pack de pony—spend all the afternoon unpack heem—a man see your night fire from stan where you waas cook your breakfast—bah!" returned Wolf-Voice.

This exasperated Ramon, who vociferated, "When I see men run the pony dat way, I was wander why dey run dem." Wolf-Voice betook himself to that ominous silence which, with Indians, follows the knife.

Ramon

Ermine was lame in the big white camp, but out here in the desert he walked ahead; so, without looking up, he removed his pipe, and said in his usual unemotional manner, "Shut up!" The command registered like a gong.

Wolf-Voice sat down and smoked. When men smoke they are doing nothing worse than thinking. The cook ceased doing the work he was paid for, and also smoked. Every one else smoked, and all watched the greatest thinker that the world has ever known—the Fire.

The first man to break the silence was the Englishman. Whether in a frock coat, or a more simple garment, the Englishman has for the last few centuries been able to think quicker, larger, and more to the purpose in hours of bewilderment, than any other kind of man. He understood that his big purpose was lost in this "battle of the kites and crows." The oak should not wither because one bird robbed another's nest. As a worldwide sportsman he had seen many yellow fellows shine their lethal weapons to the discomfiture of his plans; and he knew that in Ermine he had an unterrified adversary to deal with. He talked kindly from behind his pipe. "Of course, Ermine, I am willing to do what is proper under any and all circumstances, and we will continue this vigorous travel if you can make the necessity of it plain to me. Frankly, I do not understand why we are doing it, and I ask you to tell me."

Ermine continued to smoke for a time, and having made his mind up he removed his pipe and said slowly: "Mr. Harding, I shot Butler, and the soldiers are after me. I have to go fast—you don't— that's all."

The gentleman addressed opened wide eyes on his guide and asked in low amazement, "D—— me—did you? Did you kill him?"

"No," replied Ermine.

Rising from his seat, Mr. Harding took the scout to one side, out of reach of other ears, and made him tell the story of the affair, with most of the girl left out.

"Why did you not give him the photograph?"

"Because he said he would make me give it and drew his pistol, and what is more, I am going back to kill the man Butler—after a while. We must go fast tomorrow, then I will be where I am safe, for a time at least."

All this gave Harding a sleepless night. He had neither the power nor the inclination to arrest the scout. He did not see how the continuance of his hunt would interfere with final justice; and he hoped to calm the mood and stay the murderous hand of the enraged man. So in half-bewilderment, on the morrow, that staid traveller found himself galloping away from the arms of the law, in a company of long-haired vagabonds; and at intervals it made him smile. This was one of those times when he wished his friends at home could have a look at him.

"Say, Wolf-Voice," said he, "Ermine says he is going back to kill Lieutenant Butler sometime later."

"He says dat—hey?"

"Yes, he says that."

"Wiell den—she wiell do eet—var much, 'fraid—what for she wan kiell dose man Butler? She already waas shoot heem en the harm."

"I think Ermine is jealous," ventured Harding.

"What you call jealous?" queried the half-breed.

"Ermine wants Butler's girl and cannot get her; that is the trouble."

"Anah-a! A bag of a squaw, ees eet?" and Wolf-Voice ran out to head a packhorse into the line of flight. Coming back he continued: "Say, Meester Harding, dese woman he ver often mak' man wan' kiell some ozer man. I have done dose ting."

"Whew!" said Harding, in amazement, but he caught himself. "But, Wolf-Voice, we do not want our friend Ermine to do it, and I want you to promise me you will help me to keep him from doing it."

"'Spose I say, 'Ermine, you no kiell Meester Butler'—he teel me to go to hell, mabeso—what den?"

"Oh, he may calm down later."

"Na—Engun she no forget," cautioned the half-breed.

"But Ermine is not an Indian."

"Na, but she all de same Engun," which was true so far as that worthy could see.

"If we do not stop him from killing Butler, he will hang or be shot for it, sooner or later, and that is certain," said Harding.

"Yees—yees; deese white man have funny way when one man kiell 'nozer. Ermine ees brave man—he eese see red, an' he wiell try eet eef he do hang. No one eese able for stop heem but deese Crooked-Bear," observed the half-breed.

"Is Crooked-Bear an Indian chief?"

"Na; she ain' Enjun, she ain' white man; she come out of the groun'. Hees head eet waas so big an' strong eet were break hees back for to carry eet."

"Where does this person live?" ventured Harding.

"Where she eese lieve, ah? Where Ermine an' his pony can find heem," was the vague reply. "You no wan' Ermine for kiell deese Butler; weel den, you say, 'Ermine, you go see Crooked-Bear—you talk wid heem.' I weel take you where you wan' go een de montaign for get de grizzly bear."

"I suppose that is the only solution, and I suppose it is my duty to do it, though the thing plays havoc with my arrangements."

Later the trail steepened and wound its tortuous way round the pine and boulders, the ponies grunting under their burdens as they slowly pushed their toilsome way upwards. When Ermine turned here to look back he could see a long day's march on the trail, and he no longer worried concerning any pursuit which might have been in progress. They found their beds early, all being exhausted by the long day's march, particularly the fugitive scout.

On the following morning, Harding suggested that he and Ermine begin the hunting, since fresh meat was needed in camp; so they started. In two hours they had an elk down and were butchering him. The antlers were in the velvet and not to the head-hunter's purpose. Making up their package of meat and hanging the rest out of the way of prowling animals, to wait a packhorse, they sat down to smoke.

"Are you still intending to kill Mr. Butler?" ventured Harding.

"Yes, when you are through hunting, I shall begin—begin to hunt Butler."

"You will find your hunting very dangerous, Ermine," ventured Harding.

"It does not matter; he has got the girl, and he may have my life or I shall have his."

"But you cannot have the girl. Certainly after killing Butler the young lady will not come to you. Do you think she would marry you? Do you dream you are her choice?"

"No, the girl would not marry me; I have forgotten her," mused Ermine, as he patiently lied to himself.

"Does this maiden wish to marry Butler?" asked Harding, who now recalled garrison gossip to the effect that all things pointed that way.

"She does."

"Then why do you kill the man she loves?"

"Because I do not want to think he is alive."

The wide vacancy of the scout's blue eyes, together with the low deliberation in his peaceful voice, was somewhat appalling to Harding. He never had thought of a murderer in this guise, and he labored with himself to believe it was only a love-sickness of rather alarming intenseness; but there was something about the young man which gave this idea pause. His desperation in battle, his Indian bringing-up, made it all extremely possible, and he searched in vain for any restraining forces. So for a long time they sat by the dead elk, and Harding sorted and picked out all the possible reasons he could conjure as to why Ermine should not kill Butler, until it began to dawn upon him that he was not replying to his arguments at all, but simply reiterating his own intentions despite them. He then recalled cases in England where fists had been the arguments under a rude lover's code; only out here the argument was more vital, more insistent, and the final effect left the lady but one choice should she care to interest herself in the affair.

Resuming his talk, Harding suggested that his guide go to his own friends, who might advise him more potently than he was able, and ended by asking pointedly, "You have friends, I presume?"

"I have one friend," answered the youth, sullenly.

"Who is he?"

"Crooked-Bear," came the reply.

"Crooked-Bear is your friend; then you must listen to him; what he advises will probably be the thing to do."

"Of course I will listen to him. He is the only person in the world I care for now. I have often heard him talking to himself, and I think he has known a woman whom he cannot forget," spoke Ermine. "He will not want me to seek my enemy's life. I have talked too much, Mr. Harding. Talk weakens a man's heart. I will make no more talk."

"Well, then, my man, go to your friend; I can do nothing more," and Harding arose. They tied their meat on the saddles, mounted, and sought their camp. On the following morning Ermine had gone.

CHAPTER TWENTY

THE END OF ALL THINGS

THE HEART OF THE RIDER HUNG LIKE A LEADEN weight in his body, as he cast accustomed glances at the old trail up the mountain to Crooked-Bear's cabin. He heard the dogs bark, and gave the wolf's call which was the hermit's countersign. The dogs grew menacing at his unfamiliar scent, but a word satisfied them. A dog forgets many things about a person in a year, but never his voice. From out of a dark corner came the goblin of the desolate mountain, ready with his gun for the unwelcome, but to greet Ermine with what enthusiasm his silent forest ways had left him. For a long time they held each other's hands, while their faces lighted with pleasure; even the warmth of kindliness kindling in the scout's as he stood in the presence of one who did not seek him with the corner of his eyes.

As they built the fire and boiled the water, the old man noted the improved appearance of his protégé—the new clothes and the perfect equipment were a starched reminder of the glories of the old world, which he had left in the years long gone. He plied his questions, and was more confused to uncover Ermine's lack of enthusiasm concerning the events which must have been tremendous, and with difficulty drew the belated news of war and men and things from him. Then like the raising of a curtain, which reveals the play, the hermit saw suddenly that it was heavy and solemn—he was to see a tragedy, and this was not a play; it was real, it was his boy, and he did not want to see a tragedy.

He feared to have it go on; he shut his eyes for a long time, and then rose to his feet and put his hands on the young man's shoulders. He sought the weak gleam of the eyes in the dusk of the cabin. "Tell me, boy, tell me all; you cannot hide it any more than a deer can hide his trail in the snow. I can read your thoughts."

Ermine did not immediately reply, but the leaden heart turned slowly into a burning coal.

"Crooked-Bear, I wanted a white girl for my wife, and I shot a soldier, who drew a revolver and said he would force me to give him her picture which I had in my pocket, and then I ran away, everybody shooting at me. They may even come here for me. They want to stand me up beside the long table with all the officers sitting around it, and they want to take me out and hang me on a tree for the ravens and magpies to pick at. That is what your white people want to do to me, Crooked-Bear, and by God they are going to have a chance to do it, for I am going back to kill the man and get the girl or die. Do you hear that, Crooked-Bear, do you hear that?"

The hermit's arms dropped to his side, and he could make no sound or sign. "Sit down, be quiet, boy; let us talk more of this thing. Be calm, and I can find a reason why you will not want to stain your hands with this man's blood. When I sent you to the white men to do a man's work in a white man's way, I did not think you would lock horns with any buck you met on the trail, like the dumb things that carry their reason for being on the point of their antlers—sit down." And the long arms of the hermit waved with a dropping motion.

Ermine sat down, but by no means found his composure. Even in the darkness his eyes gave an unnatural light, his muscles twitched, and his feet were not still. "I knew, Crooked-Bear, I knew you would talk that way. It is the soft talk of the white men. She made a fool of me, and he was going to put his foot on me as though John Ermine was a grasshopper, and every white man would say to me after that, 'Be quiet, Ermine, sit down.' Bah! I will be quiet and I will sit down until they forget a little, and then—" Ermine emitted the savage snarl of a lynx in a steel trap. Slapping his knee, he continued: "The white men in the camp are two-sided; they pat you with a hand that is always ready to strike. When the girl looked at me, it lighted a fire in my heart, and then she blew the flame until I was burning up. She told me as well as any words can say, 'Come on,' and when I offered her my hand she blatted like a fawn and ran away. As if that were not enough, this Butler walked into the room and talked to me as though I were a dog and drew his gun; everything swam before my eyes, and they swim yet, Crooked-Bear. I tell you I will kill him as surely as day follows night. These soldiers talk as white and soft as milk when it suits their plan, but old Major Searles says that they stand pat in war, that they never give up the fight, that they must win if it takes years to do it. Very well, I shall not forget that."

"But, my boy, you must not see red in a private feud; that is only allowed against the enemies of the whole people. Your heart has gone to your head; you can never win a white woman by spilling the blood of the other man who happens to love her also. That is not the way with them."

"No, it is not the way with them; it is the way with their women to set a man on fire and then laugh at him, and it is the way with their men to draw a gun. What do they expect, Crooked-Bear? I ask you that!"

"Who was the girl, Ermine?"

The scout unwrapped the package from his bosom, and handed the photograph to the old man, saying, "She is like that."

The hermit regarded the picture and ventured, "An officer's daughter?"

"Yes; daughter of Major Searles."

"Who was the man you shot?"

"A young pony soldier—an officer; his name is Butler." And gradually Ermine was led to reveal events to the wise man, who was able to piece out the plot with much knowledge not natural to the wilds of the Rocky Mountains. And it was a tragedy. He knew that the girl's unfortunate shot had penetrated deeper than Ermine's, and that the Law and the Lawless were in a death grapple.

They sought their bunks, and in the following days the prophet poured much cold water on Ermine's determination, which only turned to steam and lost itself in the air. The love of the woman and the hate of the man had taken root in the bedrock of his human nature, and the pallid "should nots" and "must nots" of the prophet only rustled the leaves of Ermine's philosophy.

"He has taken her from me; he has made me lose everything I worked for with the white men; he has made me a human wolf, and I mean to go back and kill him. You say I may lose my life; ho! What is a dead man? A dead man and a buffalo chip look just alike to these mountains, to this sky, and to me, Crooked-Bear," came the lover's reply.

And at other times: "I know, Crooked-Bear, that you wanted a girl to marry you once, and because she would not, you have lived all your life like a gray bear up here in these rocks, and you will die here. I am not going to do that; I am going to make others drink with me this bitter drink, which will sweeten it for me."

Sadly the hermit saw this last interest on earth pass from him; saw Fate wave her victorious banners over him; saw the forces of nature work their will; and he sank under the burden of his thoughts. "I had hoped," he said to himself, "to be able to restore this boy to his proper place among the white people, but I have failed. I do not understand why men should be so afflicted in this world as Ermine and I have been, but doubtless it is the working of a great law, and possibly of a good one. My long years as a hunter have taught me that the stopping of the heart-beat is no great thing—it is soon over; but the years of living that some men are made to undergo is a very trying matter. Brave and sane is he who keeps his faith. I fear for the boy."

After a few weeks Ermine could no longer bear with the sullen savagery of his emotions, and he took his departure. Crooked-Bear sat by his cabin door and saw him tie his blanket on his saddle; saw him mount and extend his hand, which he shook, and they parted without a word. They had grown accustomed to this ending; there was nothing in words that mattered now. The prophet's boy disappeared in the gloom of the woods, snapping bushes, and rolling stones, until there was no sound save the crackling of the fire on the lonely hearth.

As Ermine ambled over the yellow wastes, he thought of the difference between now and his going to the white man one year ago. Then he was full of hopes; but now no Crow Indian would dare be seen in his company—not even Wolf-Voice could offer him the comfort of his reckless presence. He was compelled to sneak into the Absaroke camp in the night, to trade for an extra pony with his relatives, and to be gone before the morning. The ghostly tepees, in the quiet of the night, seemed to dance around him, coming up, and then retiring, while their smoke-flaps waved their giant fingers, beckoning him to be gone. The dogs slunk from him, and the ponies walked away. The curse of the white man was here in the shadows, and he could feel the Indians draw their robes more closely over their heads as they dreamed. The winds from the mountains blew on his back to help him along, and whispered ugly thoughts. All the good of the world had drawn away from Ermine, and it seemed that the sun did not care to look at him, so long was he left to stumble through the dark. But Nature did not paint this part of her day any blacker than she had Ermine's heart; each footfall of his pony took him nearer to death, and he whipped on impatiently to meet it. Hope had long since departed—he could not steal the girl; he realized the impossibility of eluding pursuit; he only wanted to carry Butler with him away from her. All the patient training of Crooked-Bear, all the humanizing influence of white association, all softening moods of the pensive face in the photograph, were blown from the fugitive as though carried on a wind; he was a shellfish-eating cave-dweller, with a Springfield, a knife, and a revolver. He had ceased to think in English, and muttered to himself in Absaroke. As his pony stumbled at a ford in the river, he cut it savagely with his whip—the pony which was the last of his friends—and it grunted piteously as it scrambled for its foothold.

Day after day he crawled through the rugged hills far from the places where men might be; for every one was his enemy, and any chance rifle would take away from him his vengeance. The tale of his undoing had travelled wide—he found that out in the Crow camp; Bacher-hish-a had told him that through her tears. He could trust no one; the scouts at Tongue River might be apathetic in an attempt to capture him, but they could not fail to report his presence if seen in the vicinity. Butler was probably in the middle of the log-town, which swarmed with soldiers, but it was there he must go, and he had one friend left, just one; it is always the last friend such a one has—the Night.

Having arrived in the vicinity of the post, he prowled out on foot with his only friend. It was early, for he must do his deed while yet the lights were lit. Any one moving about after "taps" would surely be investigated by the guard. The country was not yet tranquil enough to permit of laxity in the matter of sentry duty, and the soldiers counted "ten" very fast after they challenged. He had laid aside his big hat, and was wrapped in his blanket. Many Indians were about, and he was less apt to be spoken to or noticed. He moved forward to the scout fire, which was outside of the guard-line, and stood for a time in some brushwood, beyond the play of the flames. He was closely enveloped in his blanket, and although Indians passed quite near him, he was not noticed. Suddenly he heard a detail of wagons clanking up the road, and conjectured rightly that they would go into the post. He ran silently toward them, and stooping low, saw against the skyline that the cavalry guard had worked up in front, impatient to shave the time when they should reach their quarters.

It was a wood train, and it clanked and ground and jingled to the quartermaster's corral, bearing one log on the last wagon which was John Ermine and his fortunes. This log slid to the ground and walked swiftly away.

*　　*　　*　　*　　*　　*

The time for "taps" was drawing near, and the post buzzed in the usual expectation of that approaching time of quiet. A rifle-shot rang loud and clear up on the officers' row; it was near Major Searles' house, every one said as they ran. Women screamed, and Tongue River cantonment laid its legs to the ground as it gathered to the place. Officers came with revolvers, and the guard with lanterns. Mrs. Searles and her daughter were clasped in each other's arms, while Mary, the cook, put her apron over her head. Searles ran out with his gun; the shot had been right under the window of his sitting room. An Indian voice greeted him, "Don' shoot; me killi him."

"Who in h—— are you?" swore Searles, at a present.

"Don' shoot, me Ahhæta—all same Sharp-Nose—don' shoot—me killi him."

"Killi who? Who have you killed? Talk up quick!"

"Me killi him. You come—you see."

By this time the crowd drew in with questions and eager to help. A sergeant arrived with a lantern, and the guard laid rude hands on the Crow scout, Sharp-Nose, who was well known. He was standing over the prostrate figure, and continued to reiterate, "Me killi him."

The lantern quickly disclosed the man on the ground to be John Ermine, late scout and fugitive from justice, shot through the heart and dead, with his blanket and rifle on the ground beside him. As he looked through the window, he had been stalked and killed by the fool whom he would not allow to shake hands with Katherine Searles, and a few moments later, when Sharp-Nose was brought into her presence, between two soldiers, she recognized him when he said, "Mabeso, now you shake hands."

"Yes, I will shake hands with you, Sharp-Nose," and half to herself, as she eyed her malevolent friend, she muttered, "and he kept you to remember me by."

ENDNOTES

INTRODUCTION

[1] Owen Wister, "The Evolution of the Cow-Puncher," in *My Dear Wister: The Frederic Remington-Owen Wister Letters* by Ben Merchant Vorpahl (Palo Alto, Calif.: American West Publishing, 1972), 80.

[2] Frederic Remington, "Horses of the West," in *The Collected Writings of Frederic Remington*, ed. Peggy and Harold Samuels (Garden City, N.Y.: Doubleday, 1979), 14, 21.

SUGGESTED READING

ANDERSON, NANCY K. *Frederic Remington: The Color of Night.* Washington, D.C.: National Gallery of Art, 2003.

DUNLAY, THOMAS W. Wolves for the Blue Soldiers: Indian Scouts and Auxiliaries with the United States Army, 1860–90. Lincoln: University of Nebraska Press, 1982.

GROSSMAN, JAMES R., ED. *The Frontier in American Culture.* Berkeley: University of California Press, 1994.

HUTCHINSON, ELIZABETH. The Indian Craze: Primitivism, Modernism, and Transculturation in American Art, 1890–1915. Durham: Duke University Press, 2009.

JACKSON, MARTA, ED. *The Illustrations of Frederic Remington.* New York: Crown Publishers, 1970.

NEMEROV, ALEXANDER. *Frederic Remington and Turn-of-the-Century America.* New Haven: Yale University Press, 1995.

SHI, DAVID E. *The Simple Life: Plain Living and High Thinking in American Culture.* New York: Oxford University Press, 1985.

SMITH, SHERRY L. *The View from Officers' Row: Army Perceptions of Western Indians.* Tucson: University of Arizona Press, 1990.

UTLEY, ROBERT M. *Frontier Regulars: The United States Army and the Indian, 1866–1891.* New York: Macmillan, 1973.

WHITE, G. EDWARD. *The Eastern Establishment and the Western Experience: The West of Frederic Remington, Theodore Roosevelt, and Owen Wister.* New Haven: Yale University Press, 1968.

Look for the following titles, available now from
The Barnes & Noble Library of Essential Reading.

Visit your Barnes & Noble bookstore,
or shop online at *www.bn.com/loer*

NONFICTION

Age of Reason, The	Thomas Paine	0760778957
Age of Revolution, The	Winston S. Churchill	0760768595
Alexander	Theodore Ayrault Dodge	0760773491
American Indian Stories	Zitkala-Ša	0760765502
Ancient Greek Historians, The	J. B. Bury	0760776350
Annals of Imperial Rome, The	Tacitus	0760788898
Antichrist, The	Friedrich Nietzsche	0760777705
Autobiography of Benjamin Franklin, The	Benjamin Franklin	0760768617
Autobiography of Charles Darwin, The	Charles Darwin	0760769087
Babylonian Life and History	E. A. Wallis Budge	0760765499
Beyond the Pleasure Principle	Sigmund Freud	0760774919
Birth of Britain, The	Winston S. Churchill	0760768579
Birth of Tragedy, The	Friedrich Nietzsche	0760780862
Century of Dishonor, A	Helen Hunt Jackson	0760778973
Characters and Events of Roman History	Guglielmo Ferrero	0760765928
Chemical History of a Candle, The	Michael Faraday	0760765227
City of God, The	Saint Augustine	0760779023
Civil War, The	Julius Caesar	0760768943
Common Law, The	Oliver Wendell Holmes	0760754985
Confessions	Jean-Jacques Rousseau	0760773599
Conquest of Gaul, The	Julius Caesar	0760768951

Treatise of Human Nature, A	David Hume	0760771723
Trial and Death of Socrates, The	Plato	0760762007
Twelve Years a Slave	Solomon Northup	0760783349
Up From Slavery	Booker T. Washington	0760752346
Utilitarianism	John Stuart Mill	0760771758
Vindication of the Rights of Woman, A	Mary Wollstonecraft	0760754942
Voyage of the *Beagle*, The	Charles Darwin	0760754969
Wealth of Nations, The	Adam Smith	0760757615
Wilderness Hunter, The	Theodore Roosevelt	0760756031
Will to Believe and Human Immortality, The	William James	0760770190
Will to Power, The	Friedrich Nietzsche	0760777772
Worst Journey in the World, The	Aspley Cherry-Garrard	0760757593

FICTION AND LITERATURE

Abbott, Edwin A.	Flatland	0760755876
Austen, Jane	Love and Freindship	0760768560
Braddon, Mary Elizabeth	Lady Audley's Secret	0760763046
Bronte, Charlotte	Professor, The	0760768854
Burroughs, Edgar Rice	Land that Time Forgot, The	0760768862
Burroughs, Edgar Rice	Martian Tales Trilogy, The	076075585X
Butler, Samuel	Way of All Flesh, The	0760765855
Castiglione, Baldesar	Book of the Courtier, The	0760768323
Cather, Willa	Alexander's Bridge	0760768870
Cather, Willa	One of Ours	0760777683
Chaucer, Geoffrey	Troilus and Criseyde	0760768919
Chesterton, G. K.	Ball and the Cross, The	0760783284
Chesterton, G. K.	Innocence and Wisdom of Father Brown, The	0760773556
Chesterton, G. K.	Man Who Was Thursday, The	0760763100
Childers, Erskine	Riddle of the Sands, The	0760765235
Cleland, John	Fanny Hill	076076591X
Conrad, Joseph	Secret Agent, The	0760783217
Cooper, James Fenimore	Pioneers, The	0760779015
Cummings, E. E.	Enormous Room, The	076077904X
Defoe, Daniel	Journal of the Plague Year, A	0760752370
Dos Passos, John	Three Soldiers	0760757542
Doyle, Arthur Conan	Complete Brigadier Gerard, The	0760768897
Doyle, Arthur Conan	Lost World, The	0760755833
Doyle, Arthur Conan	White Company and Sir Nigel, The	0760768900

Trollope, Anthony	Warden, The	0760773610
Twain, Mark	Tramp Abroad, A	0760773629
Verne, Jules	From the Earth to the Moon	0760765197
Wallace, Lew	Ben-Hur	0760763062
Walpole, Horace	Castle of Otranto, The	0760763070
Whitman, Walt	Specimen Days	0760791139
Wells, H. G.	Island of Doctor Moreau, The	0760755841
Woolf, Virginia	Jacob's Room	0760778981
Zola, Emile	Ladies' Paradise, The	0760777675

THE BARNES & NOBLE
LIBRARY OF ESSENTIAL READING

This series has been established to provide affordable access to books of literary, academic, and historic value—works of both well-known writers and those who deserve to be rediscovered. Selected and introduced by scholars and specialists with an intimate knowledge of the works, these volumes present complete, original texts in a modern, readable typeface—welcoming a new generation of readers to influential and important books of the past. With more than 300 titles already in print and more than 100 forthcoming, the Library of Essential Reading offers an unrivaled variety of thought, scholarship, and entertainment. Best of all, these handsome and durable paperbacks are priced to be exceptionally affordable. For a full list of titles, visit *www.bn.com/loer*.